20 Sexy Stories:

Romantic, Erotic Stories For Women To Enjoy

Book Three

By Rory Richards

Copyright © 2015

Rory Richards Publishing

ISBN-10: 1518680186
ISBN-13: 978-1518680182

CONTENTS

At the Beach	1
Snuggling	8
Cooking For You	15
Springtime Lovers	23
Swimming Pool Surprise	27
Hiking Together	33
In Your Bedroom	43
Shaving For You	49
After the Costume Party	54
In Our Pajamas	61
Airport Arrival	67
Licking You	75
Night Nurse	78
My Sexy Dream About You	84

You Take Charge   87

Masturbating Together   93

Two At Once   97

Seduction Massage   104

3 AM   109

In the Backyard Hammock   115

About the Author   125

Also By Rory Richards   127

At the Beach

We pull into the parking lot at the beach. There are lots of cars here, but we know if we walk quite a ways down the beach, there'll be almost no one around.

"I bought a new bikini," you announce proudly. "and I have it on under my clothes so I won't have to change in the car."

"I can't wait to see you in it!" I say with a smile.

Carrying our little cooler full of drinks, a big beach blanket, and all of the other items one can't do without at the beach, we set out hand-in-hand to escape the crowd.

After quite a hike, we arrive at our favorite spot which lies between two dunes and out of sight of people, yet close enough to the water that we can run into the waves whenever we like.

As I spread out the beach blanket, you take off your t-shirt and cut-off jeans to reveal your new bikini.

"*Wow*! A *gold* bikini!!!" you hear me remark while looking you up and down.

"Do you like it?" you ask, even though you already know the answer.

You sit down on the big blanket and I begin to rub lotion on your back as you rub it onto your arms, legs, face, and those other places that you don't want to be burned by the sun. Then you offer to rub some lotion on my back.

After we are all oiled up and have taken a couple of cold drinks out of the cooler, we both lay down on the blanket and talk as the sun warms us. We smile at each other and kiss a bit.

When we feel really, really hot from the sun's rays, we run hand-in-hand towards the water and jump right into the waves!

You splash me in a playful way. I pretend that some salt water got into my eyes. When you move closer to see if I really am hurt, I wrap my arms around you and laugh. You laugh too when you realize that I'm faking. Then we kiss for a long time right there in the water.

I pick you up and carry you a bit farther out until the water comes up to our shoulders. At first, you hang onto me tightly, but soon realize that you can stand up on the sandy bottom. You kiss me in that special way which lets me know that you enjoy being close. Then you look towards the beach to see if anyone is watching us. They aren't.

"Kiss me again." you say over the gentle sounds of the waves.

As our lips touch, you pull down the top of your new gold bathing suit under the water and rub your breasts against my bare chest.

I can feel your nipples getting hard as they come in contact with the cool water. No one on the beach has any idea what's going on. I duck my head under the water and kiss each of your lovely nipples.

Coming to the surface again to breathe, I wrap my arms around you again and pull you towards me. You jump up in the water and wrap your legs around my waist.

Your arms are around my neck. Your bare breasts press against my chest. We're both getting turned on - warm water, bare skin, sunshine, kisses. What a beautiful day!

You slip your tongue into my mouth - and as you do, one of your hands slides down the front of my swim trunks to find that my cock is completely ready for you.

Pushing my trunks down underneath the water, you can feel my cock pressing against the front of your bikini bottom. You quickly move your whole body so that your pussy rubs against it in exactly the right place.

"I want you *so* much!" I speak for both of us.

You say nothing - just reach down, wrap your fingers around my hard cock, and move it up between your legs on the outside of your bathing suit. You're quite wet now - is it because we're in the water? Or is it because you're filled with desire?

3

The sun sparkles in your eyes as your hand moves below the water to pull the gold fabric of your bikini bottom over to one side. Your smile turns into a grin as you feel my hard cock touch the bare skin between your legs. Your fingers move it to your opening and you take just the first inch inside. Wrapping your legs even tighter around my waist, you kiss me long and hard. As we kiss, you wiggle your hips from side-to-side and take more and more of my big cock into your ready pussy.

The cool water surrounds us. No one is nearby - it's just the ocean and the two of us. As you start moving your hips in circles, my cock slips even farther inside. Still we kiss - more passionately now.

I begin to move with you and can feel your inner muscles beginning to tense up. We're making love in the water and it feels *very* special!

Putting my hands under your bottom to help support you, I begin to thrust deeper and deeper. One of your hands moves down between your legs to feel my cock going in and out. Your fingers touch your clit and begin to rub it. Now you can feel the very tip of my cock touching the back walls of your pussy.

You wrap your arms tightly around me - enjoying the feelings of being surrounded by the ocean and completely full of cock.

"Make love with me until you just *have to* cum!" I urge you.

This is all you need to hear! Your heels thump against my bottom as you slide your whole body up and down on my stiff cock. Now all of your thoughts are concentrated between your legs.

"Are you close? Are you going to cum with me, you beautiful, sexy woman?"

You say nothing, but your moans grow louder. The water feels great! I can feel your pussy muscles gripping my cock as if they may never let go. Looking down, I can see your beautiful nipples rubbing against my chest under the water, your bare legs wrapped around my waist, and your wet pussy riding me.

Our bodies tense up at the exact same moment. Your eyes open wide as you feel the first jet of cum filling your pussy.

I push my tongue into your mouth and, as you feel a second wave of my cum, your pussy muscles contract again and again. I can easily tell that you are cumming with me.

We hold each other in the water for what seems like forever - just enjoying the strong, sexy feelings. You slowly unwrap your legs from around my waist, and I help you to stand up again in the water. Your legs are a bit wobbly and so are mine.

What you do next *really* surprises me!

Ducking your head under the water, you take my still-erect cock into your mouth. Your lips wrap around it and I feel you sucking, sucking, until I cum some more. You love to taste my cum!

You suddenly realize that you need to come up for air. After you catch your breath, I kiss you and can taste our cum on your lips.

Hand-in-hand we make our way back to the shore and to our blanket. You carefully adjust your bathing suit so no one can tell what we've been doing. Finally, we reach our blanket and collapse into each other's arms.

As we lay on our backs to dry off, your eyes are sparkling in the afternoon sun. We look over at each other and realize we both have the same idea at the exact same time.

Ice cream!!! We both want ice cream!!!

Gathering our things together, we prepare to leave the beach and take one last long look at the ocean - the beautiful ocean that held us as we made love. The special ocean that wrapped around us as we wrapped our arms around each other.

"Thank you, Ocean." we say together.

Then we quickly grab all of our things and run up the beach towards the car yelling "Ice cream! Ice cream!" and naming all of our favorite flavors.

******

In a little while, we're sitting in the ice cream parlor feeding each other bites and giggling and telling each other what a perfect day it was for making love at the beach.

Snuggling

After a delicious dinner, we arrive back at your place. As you turn the key in the lock, you look at me and say. "I have a little surprise for you."

This is the first time that I've been in your home and I'm amazed by the beautiful scene that you've prepared especially for us.

In the center of your living room is a huge pile of pillows of all shapes, sizes, and colors. Surrounding them are candles everywhere - tiny candles on the shelves and a corner table, medium-sized candles on the coffee table and bookshelves, and tall candles on stands of their own in a wide circle around the pile of pillows.

"Please help me light the candles?" you ask while handing me a box of wooden matches. "Of course I couldn't leave them lit while we were out."

You remove your jacket and we take our shoes off to keep the pillows clean as we step over them. There are so many candles to light that we are soon giggling and laughing together in hushed tones.

As I touch a match to the very last candle, you go around and turn out all the lights, then come closer to me.

"Do you like it?" you ask with the

reflections of countless flickering candles in your eyes. Something about the delicate movements of the light on the walls makes you appear even more beautiful than I previously thought.

"Yes - it's delightful!" I reply - still not quite sure what your plan might be.

"I really like you." you begin. "I know it's been a long time since you've snuggled with anyone and want to make this evening very special for us."

Walking over to the stereo, you put on some instrumental music. It's music that I am familiar with - the kind that instantly speaks to our souls.

Returning to where I'm standing, you wrap your arms around my neck and whisper. "Now I'm going to show you what snuggling means to *me*!"

Your smile widens as you put your arms around me and look down, first touching your chin against my chest, then pressing your face against my dress shirt.

We're holding each other a little tighter now. With your face still held against me, you breathe in with your eyes closed. You can smell the freshly-laundered shirt that I have on, mixed with the unique scent of my body. You linger for awhile there, moving your face ever-so-slightly from side to side a couple of times to breathe me in some more.

"Mmmmm, you smell good!" you say in

a muffled voice.

I laugh and you laugh along with me. I feel your head shake against my body with each chuckle.

You look back up at my face and, without a word, gently guide me down to the pillows on the floor. In no time, we're wrapped up in each other's arms. Side-by-side we lay while slowly sinking deeper and deeper into the huge pile of pillows. Your head is snuggling onto my shoulder as you say softly. "I'm liking this even more than I imagined."

Smelling your hair, I whisper. "I'm so glad that you thought of this. I'm honored that you chose to share this special experience with me."

I feel your soft lips gently graze against my neck. It's not quite a kiss, but then, what else could it be? The feeling sends a delightful shiver up my spine and my arms instinctively wrap more tightly around you. You respond by wrapping both of your legs around one of mine and resting one hand in the center of my chest.

We look into each other's eyes again and see the countless warm reflections of the flickering candles. We're both feeling fortunate to have found each other as we kiss for the very first time.

"I'm in a very cuddly mood tonight." you whisper after our kiss.

"I'm feeling very *oral* tonight!" I tease.

"How did you guess that I *love* that?" you reply with raised eyebrows.

Rolling you over on top of me, I stroke the fingers of one hand gently up and down your spine. We're just taking our time and enjoying each other. Gently sliding my hands up the back of your short skirt and inside your panties, I can feel the wetness building between your legs. Your kisses become more and more enthusiastic.

I roll you over onto your back to kiss your nipples through your soft cashmere sweater and am delighted to find that you don't have a bra on. You feel my kisses travel farther and farther down your tummy until they reach the special place between your legs. I kiss all around the front of your panties until you move your hands down to take them off. You're feeling a bit shy, but open your legs just enough for my tongue to find your clit.

The candlelight flickers and dances as my tongue continues to turn you on. Eventually, you can't take it any more and spread your legs wide. I can see your lovely pussy by the candlelight. It's so beautiful!

I kiss up from the inside of one knee until my lips just touch your bare clit and give it a tiny kiss. Touching it with just the tip of my tongue, I give it a small lick, then a couple more licks, more firmly this time. You are rapidly getting wetter now as my tongue traces the edges of your pussy lips from the back to the front and from the front to the back - licking, licking, licking!

I whisper. "Do you like that feeling?"

You arch your back in reply as your pussy begins to involuntarily move against my tongue. My jeans are getting much too tight. I move one hand down to unzip them while still kissing and licking your pussy.

After more few minutes of enthusiastic licking, I kneel up and we help each other to take off all of our clothes. Now we're completely naked together for the first time!

I roll you over on top of me again. Your tongue slips into my mouth as your hand moves my cock to the opening of your eager pussy. Not wanting to hurt you, I let you go at your own pace. You slowly take in just the very tip.

"Oh!" you exclaim. "It's bigger than I expected!"

It's a good thing that you're already dripping wet as you take in more and more of my long, thick cock - three inches, five, seven, nine! As you feel my warm balls touch between your legs, you breathe a sigh of relief. You aren't sure you could fit another inch!

Drawing in my breath, I whisper. "Your pussy feels wonderful!"

My hands grip your bottom and help you move up and down on top of me. You begin to fuck me in earnest - slowly at first, then faster, harder, faster!

I can feel the heat building deep inside of you. You tighten your pussy muscles around my huge erection and roll me over on top of you.

"Fuck me now! Fuck me good!" I hear you demand breathlessly.

Those are the words I've been waiting to hear. I push in as far as possible and start to fuck you wildly.

You grab my rear with both hands and pull hard each time that I thrust. Knowing that you're getting close, I raise up on my arms to make longer strokes. With each deep stroke, you moan louder and louder until you start to cum! It's a good thing too, because I'm cumming with you!

You groan just a bit and then swear loudly while tossing your head from side-to-side - completely lost in a series of strong orgasms.

******

When you finally can speak again, I hear you laugh and say. "*That's* what snuggling means to me!"

We hold each other close and snuggle until we both fall asleep on the big pile of pillows.

Cooking For You

It's our third date and I've invited you over to my place for dinner. Yes, I really *am* capable of cooking a meal, and your favorite pasta dish is in progress.

"Yum, I love pasta!" you say with that sexy smile that I've grown to love.

"I'm making a marinara sauce with red wine and garlic."

"I love garlic too, but what if we want to kiss later?"

"Well, if we both eat some, that will be fine." I answer. "I have to stir the sauce again - would you like a glass of wine?"

"Oh, this is a favorite of mine - yes, please!" you say while looking at the label. "I usually don't drink more than one glass though - I'm very tactile and like to be aware of all my senses."

"Tactile?"

"You know, touchy-feely."

"Oh, so am I." I agree while pouring two glasses of wine. "Here's to you!"

Clink, sip.

"Mmmmmm, delicious!"

"I see that you have a nice, clean white blouse on - hope you don't get tomato sauce on it."

"That's what napkins are for."

"I like your face - you have a lovely

smile."

"Thank you, I really like your blue eyes!"

"I can tell that you're a fun-loving woman."

"If you play your cards right tonight, you might find out just how much fun I can be!"

"I'll try my best - would you like a lot of pasta, or a little?"

"Just a little to begin, please."

"OK, you can start on your salad if you like. Do you like your pasta rinsed - or just drained?"

"Since we're eating it right away, drained is fine."

"That's how I like it, too - it stays hot longer that way."

"Exactly."

"It's almost cooked to perfection - just a couple more minutes."

As I bend over to get a serving platter from the cupboard, I feel your eyes checking out my rear. I'm glad that I ride my bicycle a lot.

"Let me take your salad plate."

"Thank you. By the way, I notice that you have a nice butt - and nice legs, too!"

"Flattery will get you everywhere! Here's the garlic bread - would you please start on it while I stir the pasta and sauce?"

"Actually, I would prefer to watch you

cook and wait for you to join me - unless there's anything I can do to help. That garlic bread smells so good!"

"The pasta will be done in just a couple of minutes."

"Will you do me a favor?"

"Yes?"

"Would you just take a moment to kiss me? I've been watching you cook and need to feel your lips on mine."

"Certainly, but let me turn the heat down on the stove first."

We look at each other and smile. I brush my fingertips across your cheek and crouch down next to your chair. You move closer and turn your face towards mine.

I feel your silky hair as our lips meet for the first time tonight. Your eyes are so bright with interest!

You playfully lick my lips, then suck gently on my bottom lip. Turning sideways in your chair, you put one leg on either side of me as I kneel down.

At first you keep your body at a distance because you don't want to seem too eager. Our kisses become more and more energetic. Your arms move behind me and pull me closer.

"I need to feel your chest up against mine and your hands on my body now." you say matter-of-factly between kisses.

Pressing my chest against yours, I hug

you tightly.

"There's a fire in the fireplace in the living room." I whisper.

We've both completely forgotten about dinner and all that we're hearing, feeling, tasting, and smelling at this moment is each other. Hand-in-hand, we walk into the living room - dinner can wait!

"I need to feel your bare skin against mine." you say in that sexy tone that always gets my attention .

After moving the sheepskin rug over in front of the fireplace, I motion to you to lay down on your back.

You give me a look that tells me you both want and need me. I marvel at how pretty you are in your jeans and white blouse.

"I'm hungry in a *different* way now!" you declare.

I say nothing, but my huge smile speaks volumes. I was hoping to have you for dessert, but as an appetizer is even better!

You pull my shirt off over my head while checking me out. I'm glad that I lifted weights today! The way that you look at my chest makes all the effort worth it.

Your tongue starts flicking hungrily at my left nipple - licking and then sucking. Then you do the same to my other nipple. I bend forward and gently kiss your forehead.

My kisses move down to the bare skin just above the top button of your blouse. You push my head down to your left nipple and I kiss it through your blouse.

"My nipples are already hard for you." you inform me.

"Yes, my lips can feel how aroused they are!"

My fingers move to unbutton your top button. Your full breasts strain against the white cloth as I undo two more buttons and kiss the soft skin which is revealed. You undo the last two buttons yourself and open your blouse as my kisses continue. I unzip the zipper of your jeans. The pretty white lace of your panties is becoming visible.

Your fingers rapidly unbutton my jeans and pull them down.

"Please leave your panties on for just a minute?" you hear me ask.

"Yes, I will, but do you mind taking your underwear off?"

"OK, will you help me?"

Slipping a finger down either side of my boxer-briefs, you slowly lower them - watching intently as they come down. You've waited a long time for that first look at my cock. Your big grin tells me you are pleasantly surprised!

"Can we please get into a '69' position?" you whisper. "I want to kiss and suck your cock. May I please be on the bottom? There's a reason."

I change my mind and pull your panties off. You lie down on your back on the sheepskin and spread your legs in anticipation.

You say softly, but firmly. "Let me get your dick in my mouth before you begin to lick and suck on my clit, please. I don't want to cum too quickly."

Your hand grasps my hard cock and pulls it towards your lips. You suck the very tip of it - gently at first, then more aggressively. The delicious slurping noises that you're making get louder and louder.

After a couple minutes of this, I hear you say. "Now you can lick my clit. When you make me cum, I'll lose control unless I have your cock in my mouth. I love sucking cock!"

You feel my body move down between your open legs and then several gentle licks teasing your bare pussy. You spread wide to allow my tongue complete access and feel it move up between your pussy lips to find your swelling clit.

I flick my tongue against it and then suck it into my mouth. At the same time, you feel my fingers slide under your bra to lightly pinch your nipples. Still I'm licking, licking.

Your mouth feels so warm around my

cock! Your hips are moving vigorously as you make love to my tongue.

"I need to be inside of you pretty soon!" you hear me say urgently.

Grasp my long shaft with both hands, you guide my cock to the entrance of your pussy. We both hold still for just a moment, then you welcome it inside.

You feel the tip of my cock pushing and pulling in and out of your pussy to warm it up. Looking down, we both watch my cock glistening with moisture as I push and pull. My huge erection is halfway in now, but neither of us is sure if you'll be able to take it all.

As I pump your pussy, I watch your breasts bouncing inside of your lacy bra - they really need to be released. I move one hand to unfasten the front clasp. Your eyes are tightly-closed with pleasure as your bra pops open to reveal your magnificent breasts. I lower myself onto your chest and our bare nipples touch.

We're kissing again. Your delightful pussy is calling for me to cum soon. I'm trying to wait as long as possible. Your nipples brush against mine with each strong rocking motion.

You pull my body even closer and I feel a delightful warmth surrounding my shaft as your pussy gets hotter and hotter. Your orgasm starts to build as we move together as one.

Feeling my body begin to tense up, you pull hard against my hips with both hands. At last, you're able to take my huge cock all the way into your ravenous pussy as we send each other over the edge. Warm cum fills you instantly. The long string of four-letter words that escape your lips describe both of our feelings exactly.

******

When we finally recover enough to speak again, you hear me say softly. "In our hurry to make love, we forgot all about dinner!"

"That's OK - I remembered to turn off the heat on the pasta and sauce while you turned up the heat of our lovemaking." you reply. "I sure am hungry now!"

A few minutes later, we're both eating pasta naked - smiling and slurping. You take a single strand of spaghetti between your lips and slowly, slowly suck into your mouth. I respond by licking butter off my garlic bread while looking at you intently. We both know exactly what we want for dessert!

Springtime Lovers

The hint of warmth in the air and the sounds of birds chirping tell us that it's finally Spring!

We're walking together in the woods. The sun is shining brightly, yet the air is still a bit cool. We pause to sit on a huge smooth boulder that's surrounded by thick pine trees. As we lay on our backs talking softly and watching the feathery clouds pass overhead, our minds and hands begin to wander.

Soon your fingers are exploring down the front of my shorts and mine are rubbing your pussy through your cut-off jeans and panties. We're out of the cool breeze now and the sun has warmed the rock we're laying on. We turn towards each other and kiss.

"How much do you want me?" you ask.

"I want you a *lot*!" is my speedy reply.

Your impish grin tells me that you want to take control today, and I'm more than willing to let you.

"Enough to let me have my way with you?" you whisper in between kisses.

"Yes, lover!!!"

"OK, then - we'll make love *my* way today."

"Mmmmmmmm, OK, I can't wait!!!"

"C'mere, let's hug." you say while wrapping your arms around me.

You kiss me again tenderly. We feel that everything is right with the world and look at each other with love in our eyes. We're made for each other!

I place my hands on your cheeks and kiss you back. You look extra-beautiful in your cut-off jeans and a skimpy top that shows your bare midriff. Tipping your head back, you give a small shiver of delight as I kiss your neck.

I slide my hands up under your top. You respond by pressing your lace-covered breasts against my palms. My thumbs find your nipples through the lace and they firm up at my touch.

Reaching down to find the edges of your top, I pull it off over your head. You feel my lips move down your chest - kissing as they go. Kissing your tummy, your navel, and down to the button at the waistband of your cut-offs. I ask you to unbutton it.

As you undo the button of your shorts, I unzip your zipper and begin to pull them off - still kissing your tummy. Off come your shorts and panties. In a flash, you unfasten your bra and toss it into a nearby clump of grass. The warm Spring sun feels great against your bare breasts!

"I want you to be naked too!" you smile as you reach down to unbutton my shorts.

As you pull them down and off, my growing cock is happy to be free!

Leaning back on the warm, smooth rock, you spread your legs. Kneeling between them, I begin to kiss where I left off - kissing your mound of Venus and then down, down.

As my lips find your pussy, I reach up to touch your nipples. They swell with excitement as my tongue discovers your clit. I kiss it gently - it's moist and warm.

"Why don't you get on top of me?" I mumble with my mouth full. "I can lick you better that way."

I lay down on my back on the warm, smooth stone and you move up over me. As your pussy presses down onto my face, my tongue is there to greet it. Your clit is already fully hard. I take it between my lips and start to hum. You can feel the tingling vibrations on your clit. This is a new experience for you! Losing control, you begin to ride my tongue like your favorite vibrator.

I reach up to touch your nipples again as you move faster against my rigid tongue. Suddenly, I feel such a huge gush of warm cum wet soak my face! It seems as if you haven't cum in days!

"Please, I need to feel your pussy wrapped around my cock now." you hear me mumble from down between your thighs.

You move your whole body to hover over my thick cock and sloowwwwly slide down onto it. Placing your hands on my stomach for balance, you begin to ride me. I hold still and watch my stiff cock going in and out as you move your hips forward and back, then from side to side, then in circles. Your breasts are bouncing right in front of my face. We are doing the dance of love.

Your pussy muscles begin to tighten up. Yes, cum again for me, lover! Cum on my cock!

Our bodies are one now. My orgasm begins to build. You realize that I'm getting close. We're both moving furiously now - making each other hotter and hotter. You cum for a third time!

A moment later, you feel my hot sperm shooting up inside of you. Your clit is tingling, your whole lower body is feeling jolts of electricity. All of your pent-up desires are released. The birds are singing their happiest songs.

It's definitely Spring!

Swimming Pool Surprise

It's late on a hot Summer afternoon. I'm lounging on a float in the backyard pool with a tall, cool drink. The sunlight sparkles and dances on the surface of the water.

Looking up towards the main house, I see you walking across the lawn in my direction.

"Hmmm." I think to myself. "The open house must be over - here comes the realtor to tell me how it went. Damn, she's a gorgeous woman!"

******

I've wanted you since the first day that you came to look the place over and sign the contract to sell it, but so far we've kept it strictly business.

As you approach, I give you a friendly wave, You wave back - looking truly beautiful in your flowing red skirt, white blouse with lace inserts, and white high heels. The summery shade of your lipstick perfectly sets off the lovely tone of your skin.

You walk to the shallow end of the pool and stand at the top of the steps. Your big smile tells me that you have good news.

"I just wrote up an offer for the full asking price!" you exclaim, barely able to conceal your excitement.

"Wow! That's great news." I answer with a huge grin while beginning to paddle the float towards you.

"Yes," you continue. "and now I can take care of something I've been wanting to do for quite some time."

Nothing could prepare me for what happens next - you calmly begin to walk down the stairs into the pool - fully clothed!

As your white high heels disappear into the water, I stop paddling and just watch. You take another step down, then another. Your beige nylons turn darker as they become soaked. As the water comes up to your thighs, your red skirt floats on top of it for a brief moment, giving me a clear view of your lovely legs and your tiny red g-string. Still, you move seductively towards me.

The water rises above your waist and soaks your white blouse, which becomes sheer and clings tightly to your curvaceous body. The cool water has instantly hardened your nipples and I can clearly see that you aren't wearing a bra. I'm still not quite sure what's happening, but I like it!

A few more steps bring you to where I'm lying on the float. The look of surprise on my face must be a bit comical, because you break into an easy laugh. Reaching under the edge of the float, you turn it over - dumping me into the water!

Sputtering, I come to the surface. I start to say something, but your lips are already pressing against mine. Your hand delicately brushes across the front of my swimsuit below the water. My cock responds instantly. You kiss me harder and slip your fingers down the front of my bathing suit to encircle my manhood. It quickly grows even bigger from your touch.

We're both standing in water up to our chests now. You place one hand on each of my hips to help you balance in the water and kiss my neck and chest. Then your kisses travel down, down.

As your lips reach the level of the water, you push my swimsuit down around my knees, duck your head under, and take my cock into your mouth - all in one smooth motion!

You remain underwater for what seems like the longest time - sucking, sucking. Finally, your head breaks the surface. You take a deep breath - then another. Our smiling eyes meet again. Your makeup must be waterproof, because you look even more beautiful than before.

Unable to wait any longer, you rip your

blouse open! A couple of buttons pop off and disappear into the water. Your bare nipples are hard as diamonds as you press them against mine.

Next, I watch you grab the front of your stockings with both hands and rip them to shreds. I'm quite surprised at how aggressive you are, but I like it!

Jumping up in the water, you encircle my waist with your strong legs. My hands instinctively move to support your rear. Your shoes have come off and are somewhere on the bottom of the pool.

Feeling my hard cock pressing against the front of your g-string, you quickly move one hand down and pull the thin strip of red satin to one side.

"I need you to make love to me!" you say in a voice dripping with desire. "I've waited *much* too long for this moment. Make love to me *right here, right now*!"

As you say this, your tongue presses into my mouth again. I can't wait any longer - my hands give a strong downward push on your hips and my cock easily slips inside of you. You feel terrific!

With your arms around my neck and your legs around my waist, I walk through the water to the steps with my cock still inside of you. You seem to enjoy these movements and begin to make sexy purring sounds.

Gently I ease you back until you're

lying on the top step - half in and half out of the water. The look on your face is one of pure pleasure. I help you to take off your wet, torn blouse. Then you unzip the side zipper of your soaked red skirt and toss it up onto the lawn.

Now you only have on your torn nylons and your red g-string. You have me so worked up that I just tear them both off. Your eyes are bright with desire. I look down at your breasts. Tiny beads of water are clinging to them. Looking farther down, I can see your pink pussy lips still wrapped around my hard cock.

"I've been waiting so long for this day - please make me cum!" you whisper.

As I lean forward, you arch your back. Your breasts rise to meet my chest. I begin to forcefully fuck you as you move your hips wildly from side-to-side. Your breathing is getting heavier now. So is mine. You gyrate your whole lower body around my big cock, then, in a burst of pure passion, dig your fingernails into my back.

Your pussy is so hot now! Your cum flows as you frantically mumble into my ear. "Oh! Yes! Yessssss!!!!!"

My cum begins to rise for you. Sensing this, you open your legs as wide as possible. I push even harder and deeper - pumping, thrusting. We both moan loudly as we cum at the same time.

Our bodies melt into a puddle of passion and pure pleasure. We look into each other's eyes and kiss again. Your pussy quivers with delight as it responds to another huge spurt of my cum.

******

As we lay in each other's arms in the warm sunlight, we're both totally relaxed, totally satisfied. The waves that our intense love-making has stirred up in the pool slowly fade away.

"Now I realize what that saying is all about. You know - business before pleasure?" you giggle.

We both laugh.

I carry you to the shower in the pool house where we wash each other and then have wild sex again. Twice.

Hiking Together

It's our first date. We're hiking together on a trail that leads to the top of a big hill where we'll be able to see for miles. We've brought a blanket and a picnic lunch to share.

I'm carrying everything so it's easier for you to walk. My small backpack might also hold a surprise or two.

It's not too hot today, but we need to stay hydrated while hiking, so I've brought both ice tea and orange juice to quench our thirst.

"Please take my hand while we climb this steeper part of the trail?" I ask politely. "My legs are longer and steadier than yours."

"That's for sure!" you say as you gladly grab my hand and we scramble up the steep trail.

"You can set the pace and we'll stop at the next fallen log to take a break. C'mon - it's only a little bit farther."

Arriving at the log, we sit close to each other. I want to kiss you, but you are out of breath, so we make ourselves content with studying each other's faces.

You have a healthy glow from all the exercise, and it's clear that you're enjoying yourself out here in nature. I can't really tell your thoughts, but you are smiling and that's always a good sign.

Our eyes turn to the spectacular view of the mountains, green grass, and far-away trees. The fresh morning air and the sweet smells of the wildflowers in bloom almost overwhelm our senses.

Because it's a warm day, you have on shorts and a short-sleeved shirt. I'm wearing jeans and a t-shirt.

As we sit, I confess to you that I've been watching your cute butt swing back and forth as you climbed the trail in front of me. You seem to be a bit shy about that so I stand up, turn around, and say. "It's OK - here, you can feel *my* butt if you like." You laugh and give it a playful squeeze. It's much tighter than you thought it would be because of all the hiking and bike riding that I do.

I sit back down next to you and bring my lips near yours - waiting to see if you will kiss me. You must have caught your breath because you begin to smother me with kisses. I like it!

While your lips are busy, you slip one hand underneath my t-shirt to feel my strong chest.

"Do you like what you feel?" I ask between kisses.

"Yes - very much!"

"It's only a little ways to the top of the hill and a beautiful view that goes on forever, shall we keep walking?"

This time you ask me to walk in front so that you can check out my butt. I'd much rather walk next to you and hold your hand, but do what you ask. After a few steps, I turn around quickly and catch you looking. You giggle and I laugh.

In a few more minutes we arrive at a little clearing at the top of the hill that's covered with thick, green grass. We spread out the blanket and sit down close to each other. The view is incredible! We can see for miles.

Leaning closer, I whisper into your ear. "Ice tea or orange juice?"

You laugh because you thought I was going to whisper something more romantic. I pour each of us a cup of cold ice tea. We clink our cups together and drink. That sure tastes great after our hike!

You look at me and stick out your tongue in a teasing way. I stick mine out too, and touch the tip of it to yours. Both of our tongues are cool from the ice tea. Turning towards me, you put your arms underneath mine, pull me closer, and kiss me. Mmmmmm - so you *do* like me!

The next thing I know, you are moving to sit in my lap facing me. As we kiss again, you wrap your arms loosely around my waist. I slip my hands an inch or two inside the waistband of your shorts to feel the bare skin there. You seem to like it.

You start moving your hips from side-to-side as we kiss - rubbing the front of your shorts against me. I'm beginning to get turned on from your movements. You seem to realize my urgent need to rearrange a certain body part and raise yourself up just for a moment. With one hand I make the necessary adjustments. You smile and sit back down in my lap. Now you can feel my rapidly-hardening cock pressing against your pussy through your shorts.

Reaching down, you unzip your zipper, then boldly reach for mine. You're pleasantly surprised to find that I don't have any underwear on. Your kisses have turned me on so much that my cock pops right out!

After kissing me hard again, you say. "May I make a request?"

"Yes, please do."

"Can I suck your cock? That *really* turns me on!"

I'm a bit surprised to hear you being this forward, but smile and nod my head in agreement.

You whisper that you'd like me to stand up, then you move off my lap and get down onto your knees on the blanket.

As I stand, you hurriedly pull my jeans down around my ankles, and before I know it, your warm lips are wrapped around my cock. You can taste it and feel it growing in your mouth as you start to suck.

Your fingers slip inside of your unzipped shorts, then inside of your panties. While taking as much of my cock into your mouth as you can, your fingers begin to rub your clit.

Looking up, you notice that my eyes are closed. This lets you know that you're definitely turning me on!

One of your hands is wrapped around my thick shaft and the other is unbuttoning your shirt to let your bare breasts feel the warm Summer sun. After setting your lovely breasts free, your fingers return to massaging your hard little clit. All this time, you are sucking my big cock as you cup my balls in your hand.

I begin to move my hips back and forth - fucking your mouth. Do you like that feeling, lover? Do you enjoy having your mouth full of cock? Does it turn you on to know that you can make a man so hot?

Kneeling up a bit, you begin to rub the tip of my stiff cock against your left nipple to make it aroused. You rub it against your other nipple until it's also aroused, then suck it back into your hot mouth.

Looking down, I can see that you have two fingers deep inside of your wet pussy - getting it ready. When you are right on the very edge of your first orgasm, you quickly stand up, pull down your shorts and panties, and kneel down on the blanket.

"Fuck me from behind!" I hear you say breathlessly.

"First I want to lick your pussy."

"Oh yes!!! Please do! I want you to eat my pussy like you missed breakfast! That makes me feel like a wild woman!"

Turning over onto your back, you watch my tongue come closer and closer. Your fingers spread your pussy lips and you moan loudly as you feel my tongue slip inside. You tense up almost immediately and it's not long before you start to cum.

"Ohhh, I love it!!!" you gasp with delight. "If I knew you could eat me out like *that*, I would have let you do it sooner!"

"Do you like that feeling, lover? Does it make you hot?" I mumble with my mouth full. "Your cum tastes great!"

Now you have one hand wrapped around my cock - stroking it and making me want to fuck you. You feel one of my fingers slip inside of your wet, wet pussy. Still I'm licking, licking.

"I need you to fuck me *really* hard from behind now!!!" you exclaim as you turn over again onto your hands and knees. One of your hands pulls my cock towards your cum-soaked pussy. You're so turned on that you just grab it and push the first 3 inches inside.

I push deeper. Your hand is still wrapped around my shaft so I can't get too far in until you feel completely ready. After a few more strong thrusts, you take your hand away and allow me to drive almost all of my huge erection deep into your pussy.

"Ohhhh!! Deeper!!!" you moan. "Fuck me good!!!

You are such a hot woman! I want to make you cum again! You begin to fuck me back.

Now I'm thrusting harder and harder and you feel my big cock filling every corner of your pussy. You are moaning so loudly that it's a good thing there's no one else around.

We're on top of the hill on our lovemaking blanket. There's no place we'd rather be. You are squeezing your pussy muscles tight with each deep thrust.

"I want you to cum again. I *need* to hear you cum - that makes me so hot!"

I can feel you moving frantically underneath me as you get closer and closer to another orgasm. Let me feel you cum, lover! Squeeze my cock tight with your pussy as you do!

We're like wild beasts fucking in the forest - a man and a woman with animal desires for each other. Cum for me!

Reaching one hand up between your legs, you rub your clit furiously as I fuck you harder and harder. I can feel your whole body tense up as you get closer and closer to one of your most powerful orgasms ever.

You hear me whisper "You made my cock huge, lover! You sucked it and made it hard, then spread your legs for my tongue until you couldn't wait any longer to feel me fucking you. Are you going to cum for me again?"

You open your mouth to speak, but nothing comes out. Your orgasm is so intense that for a couple of minutes, you are unable to move. I try to thrust in and out, but your pussy is gripping my cock so tightly that I couldn't pull it out if I wanted to! My fingers reach for both of your nipples and squeeze them as your whole body shivers with pleasure.

When you finally regain a bit of control, I hear you say in a voice that sounds far away. "Please put that big cock of yours back into my mouth and fuck it as if it was my pussy."

As you say this, you turn around and take my cock into your mouth while offering your dripping pussy to my tongue again. You suck hard as I lick you faster and faster. Your mouth is full of my cock and my mouth is full of your pussy! You are grinding your whole pussy against my face now while I aggressively fuck your throat. Your clit is so hard. Your pussy is *so* wet! You can taste a tiny bit of my pre-cum begin to ooze out, and begin anticipating that huge gush that you love so much. You open your throat to allow even more of my huge cock in - and suddenly, you get what you've been waiting for. A spurt of thick cum fills your mouth. Then another! You swallow some to get ready for the next big spurt.

"Do you like that taste, lover? Do you like the taste of my cum? *You* did that! *You* made me cum! Cum on my tongue now! I need to taste your cum! Fuck my tongue while you suck my cock!"

Finally, I taste another warm trickle of your cum too. Yes, swallow my cum as I swallow yours!

You swallow again. My cum fills your mouth for a second time as yours runs down my chin.

Quickly sitting up, you push me down onto my back on the blanket and take my cock back into your pussy again - fucking me as we kiss. We're enjoying each other's naked bodies, pleasuring each other as a man and a woman are made to do - satisfying our primal urges right here in the woods as our ancestors once did.

A cool breeze surrounds our hot bodies as we lay on our love blanket - kissing and making love slowly and tenderly now.

You relax completely on top of me. I can't see your face, but know that you are smiling.

I whisper. "What a delicious first date this is!"

"Yes, I can hardly wait for our second date!"

In Your Bedroom

"Let me know when you feel sleepy, OK?" you hear me say as we snuggle together on the couch.

"I'm ready now - will you tuck me in?"

"Yes, I already lit some candles in the bedroom and will carry you up when you're ready."

"Let's go now - I can't stop yawning."

"OK, I'm sleepy too, and we both have to work tomorrow."

The next thing you know, I'm picking you up and carrying you down the long hallway. As we climb the stairs, I feel your luscious kisses on my neck.

"Hey, quit kissing my neck! I might stumble and hurt us both!" I laugh.

You behave yourself (kind of) as we continue towards the bedroom. The scented candles smell wonderful as we walk in. Lights and shadows are dancing on the ceiling.

I stand you up by the side of the bed. Your arms are still around my neck. I see the reflections of the candles in your eyes as we kiss again.

You press your chest against mine. I can feel your nipples swelling with desire through my thin t-shirt. You toss your head back to allow me to kiss your neck -

first one side, then the other.

I help you to lie down on your pillow. You are so attractive by candlelight! We kiss again, then you push my head down until my lips touch your chest. I kiss your left nipple through your pajama top. Closing your eyes, you tip your head back again in pleasure as you feel my warm lips surround your right nipple through the soft flannel.

Your fingers move to undo the top button of your pajamas, then the next - and the next. Unbuttoning the last button, you open your pajama top and feel my lips kiss your bare nipples for the first time tonight.

Leaning back onto the bed, you get more comfortable. I kiss your smooth tummy while cupping your breasts with my warm hands.

Softly, gently, you feel my kisses travel down until they reach the waistband of your pajama bottoms. Now my lips are *almost* where you need them to be.

Placing your hands on top of mine, you sigh a beautiful sigh, move your hips towards me a bit, and open your legs in a clear invitation. I kiss down, down, down. As my mouth finds the small wet spot that has been forming, you arch your back in pleasure.

My tongue presses against your pussy now - firmly, yet gently. Your hands pull at the waistband of your pajama bottoms. I lean back just enough to let you take them off. At the same time, I remove my t-shirt and move my bare chest back between your legs.

You playfully squeeze me with your legs, then open them as a signal that I should continue. You give a loud moan as you feel my kisses arrive at your opening, then lick up until my tongue finds your aroused clit. I begin to gently flick it with my tongue, then kiss it full-on and suck it into my mouth. Your clit is completely aroused now and your juices are flowing as you press your pussy firmly against my face. My tongue slips inside to pleasure you. You taste delicious!

Getting hotter and hotter, you pull me up so we can kiss again. As you do, you feel my hard cock pressing between your open legs and straining to be released from my pants.

You quickly unzip my jeans and reach inside. Your fingers feel great wrapped around my stiff cock! I push my jeans down and off. Now we are naked together.

Grasping my cock, you pull it towards you. When it's right at the entrance to your pussy, you touch it to your clit and move just the very tip up and down against it - over and over again. Then you moan again, push it down and guide the tip inside. You are so wet!

Moving your pussy in small circles, you walk your hips towards me. With each movement, you take in more cock - 3 inches, 6 inches, all 9 inches!

You look at me expectantly as I begin to pump your pussy hard and fast. Your hard nipples brush against mine with every deep stroke. Your eyes are closed and you're breathing heavily. Sleep will have to wait!

I continue to pump - pulling all but one inch out and slooooowly pushing back in - all the way in. You grip my ass tightly with both hands and squeeze it to show me the rhythm that you desire. I can tell you're getting close because you're pushing back each time I thrust. I'm as hard for you as you are wet for me. Your eyes are closed and you're breathing heavily.

I whisper in your ear. "May I please cum inside of you tonight?"

"Mmmmmm! Please do!"

"Will you cum with me?"

"Oh, yes, you *know* I will!"

Your eyes sparkle in the candlelight as you lock me in with your legs. With each of our movements, your pussy grips my thick cock even tighter. I begin to stroke faster. Your face looks angelic as your lips part and you give a small moan, then a larger one as the first wave of your cum surrounds my throbbing cock. So wet! So warm!

You are wildly kissing my neck. I hold still as you grind your pussy against my cock while your inner muscles contract in extreme pleasure. Wiggling your hips excitedly, you soon feel the first surge of my cum mixing with yours.

Pulling all the way out, I rub the tip of my cock against your wet clit. The second wave of my cum sprays directly against it. We hold like that for a brief moment, then I roll you over on top of me. As I look at your beautiful body in the candlelight, you start to ride me. I reach up to pull on your nipples.

In no time, you're cumming wildly and crying out over and over again.

"Fuck! Fuck!! Fuck!!! Ohgodyes!!!!"

You are dizzy with pleasure and I can feel our warm juices flowing down around my balls and onto the sheets. Still you excitedly rotate your pussy around my stiff cock to experience every possible bit of pleasure.

When you're 100% satisfied, you lean forward and collapse onto my body with my cock still inside of you.

Pulling the blankets up over both of us, you whisper. "Can we please try to sleep like this?"

"Yes, definitely!"

After leaning over to blow out the candles on the bedside table, you snuggle into my arms.

I kiss your forehead, then your eyes, then your lips.

You rest your head on my shoulder - so sleepy, so satisfied, *such* a woman!

Shaving For You

"I woke up *extremely* horny this morning!" you announce with a huge grin on your face. "Let's make love!"

"My prickly beard might feel uncomfortable on your sensitive skin, so I should shave first." is my reply.

"Mmmmmmmm - I love watching a man shave!" you say with an even bigger smile. "I'll sit on the bathroom counter and watch you."

We move into the spacious bathroom. Taking off my pajama top, I lather up my face and make eye contact with you in the mirror. You watch intently as I concentrate on that tough-to-shave spot on my chin.

"C'mon, let's hop into the shower when you're done." you tease. "I *might* just do something *special* for you!"

You walk over to turn on the water in the shower. It steams up the mirror just as I finish shaving. I take off my pajama bottoms as you slip off your robe to reveal your matching pink bra and panties.

"Let me undress you, please?"

"Of course you can!"

I sit on the edge of the tub with my face just above panty level.

"Come closer and let me smell your

49

sexy smells."

You slowly move towards me. Reaching behind you, I grasp your beautiful bottom with both hands and pull you closer to my hungry lips and tongue. You place both hands on my shoulders for balance.

I playfully kiss your belly button. With a sense of urgency, you pull your panties down to reveal your glorious pussy. I love the way that it looks just before I tongue you - moist, but still closed, with just a hint of pink.

After you step out of your panties, I return my hands to your ass and pull you towards me again. You perch one foot up on my shoulder to allow my lips and tongue total access to your pussy. Feeling my first kiss on your naked clit, you let out a soft moan of pleasure.

"Your lips feel wonderful!" you remark. "If you lick my clit, I'll cum quickly!"

You must be exceptionally horny because in less than 60 seconds an intense orgasm is building. Looking up, I see your breasts straining to get out of that pink bra. Your nipples are firm with arousal.

Still I lick while reaching behind you to unhook your bra. It falls onto the floor, and you stand naked before me. A shiver of desire flows throughout your whole body.

"Let's get into the shower now." you say anxiously.

The water temperature is just right. Looking down to see that I'm fully erect for you, a smile of anticipation comes over your face.

"How would you like it this morning?" you hear me ask over the sounds of the running water. "How about from behind while standing up?"

Still smiling, you turn around to face the wall, then snuggle back up against me. The warm water makes us feel even closer. I slip my hard cock between your legs so you can see the tip of it poking out the front. This always makes you hot! You start rubbing your pussy along the whole length of my shaft.

Unexpectedly, the tip of it slips inside! I suddenly feel an urgent need to push *all* the way in and pull your whole body towards me - probing the depths of your soaking wet pussy. Our bodies fit together perfectly as if they were made for each other.

Leaning forward, you put both hands on the wall as I thrust both fast and deep. Looking down, I see your pussy enveloping my cock and start fucking you hard while squeezing your nipples with my fingers.

Your orgasm takes you by surprise! Reaching back with both hands, you grab my ass and pull me as close as possible.

Your pussy muscles are massaging my cock while you enjoy a beautiful, intense orgasm.

"Please turn around so I can kiss you?" you hear me ask.

You turn and take me in your arms. Your lips are hungry for mine. We share long, deep, luxurious kisses.

I pick you up off the shower floor and slip my cock back in while you wrap your legs around my waist. Now I'm bouncing your whole body up and down on my rock-hard cock. You love it!

You are still kissing me and excitedly sucking on my lips and tongue. I feel my orgasm building. Yes, let's cum together this time! Squeeze my cock with your pussy muscles while I cum inside of you!

This time you have a cluster of amazing orgasms. Your pussy muscles clamp down on my cock as if they'll never let go!

"Damn! Damn!! You fuck me so *good*!!!" you cry out with pleasure.

******

When you've finally calmed down and we've rinsed ourselves off, I turn off the shower and reach for a huge towel to dry us both. You snuggle up against me as I towel off your sexy body.

"You really tired me out! Now I need a

nap." you announce.

Picking you up again, I carry you into the bedroom, set you down on our bed, and gaze into your eyes. You reach up to caress my cheek, then kiss me full on the lips. It's a sweet kiss of thanks.

We're both clean and satisfied. You drift off to sleep and have a beautiful dream about us making love while I get dressed and ready to go to work.

After the Costume Party

We met at the big costume party and hit it off right away. You were dressed as the sexiest nurse that I've ever seen!

After a long evening of drinking, dancing, and making out, you finally decided to invite me to come home with you.

******

We arrive at your place and, after you've made us some refreshing drinks, we're sitting on the couch talking.

"I couldn't help but notice that you have lovely nipples." I say. "I tried not to look, but..."

"You did *not* try not to look, just tried not to *look* like you were looking." you laugh. "Well, you ain't seen nothing yet!"

"I would really like to kiss them through your nurses' costume and make them aroused." I tease. "After a few kisses, you might want to feel my lips directly on them."

"There is *way* too much fabric here for me to feel your kisses the way I need to." you say while starting to undo the buttons of your blouse. "Kiss my lips instead."

I gladly comply. Between kisses, I

glance down to see your lovely breasts being uncovered. They look so sexy wrapped in that white lace bra! You unfasten the last button and give me a look that says you just might eat me alive. I can't think of a better way to go!

I try to kiss your neck, but your hair gets in the way, so you brush it aside with your fingers to allow my lips full access.

After a couple of minutes, you abruptly pull your bra up over the top of your breasts and push my head down towards your chest. Leaning forward, you press your right nipple against my lips and feel me suck it into my mouth. After a minute or so, you place one palm on each side of my face and move my mouth over to the other nipple. Sliding forward on the sofa, you hike up your white nurse's skirt to expose your sexy white nylons. I can see that you don't have any panties on under them.

"Lick my pussy *now*!" you say impatiently as you raise your hips and begin to pull your nylons down - and off. I'm more than happy to help you to do that.

"I want to make you cum with my tongue." you hear me say.

"Yes, I need you to make me cum!" you say while quickly removing your bra and the rest of the nurses' outfit. Now you are completely naked - and even more lovely with your clothes off.

"Let's do a '69' on the floor." you suggest.

I lie down on my back on the rug and you hover over me. Our lips meet. As we kiss, I feel your fingers undoing the buttons on my pants, slip inside my black boxer-briefs, and touch my rapidly-hardening cock for the first time ever. Your other hand unzips my zipper - and just in time, too!

"I like a warm cock in my hand." you say with a playful grin while stroking it lovingly.

Before I realize it, you've turned around and your full lips are wrapped around my cock as you place one leg on each side of my head.

You slowly lower your pussy towards my ready tongue. At first contact, you tense up for just a second, then take even more of my cock into your mouth. As you do, you lower your pussy farther onto my waiting tongue.

Now we're both licking, sucking, sucking, licking. Each of us is lost in pleasuring the other. In and out goes my tongue. I can tell that you're getting close to cumming because of the way that you're hungrily sucking my cock. Your clit is swollen, hot, and pulsating. You can feel my cock throbbing in your mouth. We both are still wildly licking and sucking.

My body tenses up - and so does yours. I hold perfectly still as you move your whole lower body up and down with great urgency. Fuck my face, lover, while you suck my cock!

Suddenly, the feeling of your warm, wet lips is more than I can take. Cum races up my shaft, and you feel the first gush fill your mouth. You suck even harder as the taste of my salty-sweet cum sends you past the point of no return.

You are riding my tongue faster now - almost there! Taking as much of my cock into your mouth as you can, you feel a huge spurt of cum hit the back of your throat. You swallow hard.

Wrapping your hand around the base of my shaft again, you stroke it rapidly. You can feel it throbbing between your wet fingers while my frantic kisses cover every inch of your pussy and clit. Your short, quick breaths are getting closer and closer together.

All of a sudden, you stop breathing, press your pussy down firmly against my face, and just hold there, motionless. Yes, you horny woman, cum on my tongue! A few more strong licks and a wave of cum flows out of your pussy. I can taste it - it's heavenly!

"I need your cock inside me while I cum some more!" you say while changing positions.

In no time, you've turned around to mount me and notice that my huge erection is pointing straight up towards the ceiling. Knowing that you have the ability to arouse me like that gives you a sense of feminine power.

Grasping my thick shaft, you guide my cock directly to your dripping pussy and swiftly lower yourself down onto it.

"Don't move, let me do it all!" you insist.

I lie perfectly still as you ride me like a rodeo rider. Fuck me, lover! Fuck me good!

Holding completely still, I can feel the heat between your legs rapidly increasing. Your hot pussy wants my cock so much! Your eyes are tightly closed as you fuck me fast and hard - getting ready to cum again.

I look up to admire your beautiful, womanly body. Your nipples are erect and proud. Your smooth skin is glowing. Your hips gyrate wildly as you fuck me. Damn, you're going to make me cum again! Do you want to feel my cum soak the back walls of your pussy? Just fuck me a little bit more and you will!

Still you move up and down, up and down. I can feel each ridge of your pussy muscles sliding over the head of my cock - milking me until I can't take it any more!

You press *all* the way down onto my

immense erection - taking all of it inside for the very first time. As you do, a huge stream of my cum warms you from the inside out. You feel it oozing out of your pussy and running down your inner thighs. The additional wetness helps you to fuck me even more rapidly. Gripping my upper arms tightly while rocking your hips back and forth fiercely, you get ready to cum again.

"Cum for me, lover! Wash my cock with your cum!"

This is exactly what you want to hear. Seconds later, you squeal with delight as another powerful cluster of orgasms overtake your senses.

******

You slowly relax on top of me as I lightly stroke my fingertips up and down your spine. Then I slide them between your legs from behind to feel where your well-fucked pussy is wrapped around my still-hard cock.

Your pussy is still fucking me - much more tenderly now as we share prolonged kisses.

After a few more moments, you rest your head on my shoulder and relax.

"Would you like to sleep on top of me for a while?" I whisper.

"Yes, let's take a nap with your cock

inside of me." you suggest while playfully squeezing me between your cum-soaked thighs.

Your bare skin feels wonderful against my body. Your breathing becomes more gentle.

"I'm not really a nurse, you know." you mumble as you drift off to sleep.

In Our Pajamas

We're sitting on the sofa watching TV in our pajamas.

"This show is boring!" you announce as you grab the remote and click off the TV. "Let's fool around instead!"

Moving closer to me, you playfully put your hand on the front of my dark blue pajama bottoms. You have on a loose pajama top with a bra underneath and white cotton panties.

I lean over and begin kissing your neck just below your ear. Your hair smells wonderful! You can feel my warm breath, then my lips gently pulling on your earlobe. You giggle and turn your face towards mine.

As our lips come closer, I stop only inches away to tease you. Unable to wait any longer, you pull my head within reach. Our lips touch and we feel a spark. Wrapping your arms around me, you whisper. "You sure know how to unleash my wild side!"

Pushing me firmly against the back of the sofa, you put one leg on each side of my body. Still we kiss - hungry, hot kisses! I can feel the warmth between your legs pressing against the front of my pajama bottoms. Taking my hands in yours, you gently place them over your breasts outside your pajama top, and move your chest forward against my palms. As you do, you begin to move your hips back and forth across my lap - back and forth, back and forth. Each time, you push down a little bit harder.

Your eyes are closed now as you move my hands up underneath your pajamas and guide my palms to the front of your black satin bra. I can feel that one of your nipples is poking out the top of your bra cup. Touching the tip of my finger to it ever-so-gently, I feel it grow harder.

Quickly unbutton your pajama top, you take it off. Before I know it, you're pressing your satin-covered breasts against my lips. My mouth finds the nipple that's poking out. I kiss it softly, suck on it, then slowly uncover your other nipple by pulling your bra cup down. Soon you feel my lips kissing and sucking that one too.

The warm spot between your legs is getting hot now - and wet too! You are pressing down more forcefully against my swiftly-growing cock.

"You love to ride up and down my shaft and feel it rub across your clit through your panties, don't you?

"Yes - doing that makes me *very* horny!"

You also enjoy knowing that it was *you*

who made my cock so big, and who made me want you so much.

Taking off your bra, you toss it over your shoulder without looking and press your bare breasts against my face again. As you do, you reach inside my pajamas. Wrapping your fingers around my hard cock, you tilt it up until the tip touches the front of your damp panties and start to playfully grind your pussy against my erection.

"I want to suck it now!" you announce with a big grin. "Your cock always tastes so *good*!"

Moving sideways on the sofa, you pull my pajama bottoms down a few inches and lower your head into my lap. I look down to watch your lips wrap around my shaft. Damn, that feels great!!!

I can also see that your fingers are busy between your legs - teasing your clit while you suck. My fingers pull gently on your bare nipples as you suck.

After a few minutes, I whisper. "I *really* need to be inside of you now."

You sit in my lap facing me again and position your hips so the tip of my cock is pressing against your pussy opening through your soaking-wet panties. Then you begin to tease me by pushing down onto it. The thin cotton of your panties only allows an inch or so to push inside of you. This feeling makes both of us even hornier!

Reaching down and moving your panties aside, you whisper. "Now *I'll* make love to *you!*"

I feel the tightness of your pussy opening encircling the tip of my cock. Wetting your fingers with your tongue, you move them down between your legs to lubricate my shaft. You press down again and the head of my thick cock slides in just a couple of inches.

You gasp. It's bigger than you remember! Still you need to fuck me. You begin to move up and down very slowly. Each time you move down, you're able to take in a bit more of my big cock.

"Damn!!! You're *huge* tonight!" I hear you say through clenched teeth. "It's going to be a while before I can fit all of *that* into my pussy!"

"I'll be gentle and not try to thrust it all in before you're ready."

You wet your fingers again, run them around the base of my shaft, and push down even farther. I'm half-way inside of you now.

"Do you need to make it wetter?" I ask." I don't want to hurt you."

You quickly move your whole body down and hungrily suck my cock into your mouth again.

I whisper. "Yes, make it really wet!"

Looking up, you see my eyes are closed

and a look of extreme pleasure on my face. One of your hands is wrapped around my shaft and the other is feeling my balls. You can feel my cock throbbing between your lips as you suck. Your fingers make your pussy wetter and wetter.

"If you keep sucking like that, I'm going to cum!!!" I exclaim.

You don't stop - in fact, you suck even harder and faster!

My breathing is becoming heavier now - and so is yours. Two of your fingers are going in and out of your pussy while your mouth pleasures my cock. Without warning, you feel a huge spurt of my cum fill your mouth!

You slip another finger into your pussy and begin to move all three of them around in a frenzy while wetting my whole cock with your mouthful of cum. Now you feel ready to take the whole thing.

Standing up, you quickly take off your panties, move into my lap, and straddle me again face-to-face. Placing my cum-covered cock at your opening, you look down to watch it easily slip into your pussy.

You are *much* wetter now. I can't help myself and ever-so-slowly push all the way in - deeper and deeper until your tight pussy is completely filled with cock. Squeezing your legs around my torso, you begin to move your hips from side-to-side.

Giggling, you say. "Now *I'm* going to fuck *you!*"

"Yes! Fuck me *good!*"

We both look down to watch my cock going in and out as you get closer and closer to orgasm. I can feel your pussy muscles starting to contract.

Losing control, you fuck me fast and hard. As your pussy muscles clamp tightly around my shaft, you begin to make those beautiful sounds that tell me you're cumming. Your wet warmth flows around my cock.

"I'm going to cum with you!" I loudly declare.

Your body goes still with anticipation. A great river of cum races up my shaft and sprays deep, deep inside of you. Closing your eyes, you feel the hot wetness filling your cum-drenched pussy. Your complete attention is focused between your legs.

******

When you're finally calmed down enough to relax, you give me that special look which can mean only one thing - total satisfaction.

We snuggle up close - skin to skin, and realize just how lucky we are!

Airport Arrival

I'm flying into the airport near your town and you're going to pick me up. Although we've chatted for a long time on the internet, exchanged photos, and talked on the phone (we even had phone sex once!), we've never met before. You're feeling just a bit apprehensive about it and have questions in your mind:

Will I be the sort of man that you imagined?

Will I be kind and easy-going?

I'm also a bit nervous and have some questions, too:

Will she be shy?

Will she want me as much as I already want her?

******

Now the time for wondering has passed. I walk past the security checkpoint and out into the public area. Not seeing you anywhere, I walk on a bit, hoping to spot you. As I pass one of the huge pillars that hold up the roof, you step out - smiling.

I laugh.

You laugh.

I say. "You *are* smart, aren't you?"

You smile even more. I've know that I've passed your initial inspection from behind the pillar.

"And what if you hadn't liked what you saw?" I ask as we hug for the very first time.

You say nothing - we both know that if you weren't attracted to me, you'd be long gone by now. As we hug, I smell your hair - mmmmmm, coconut! My hands politely rest at the small of your back.

It's too soon for us to kiss - we both know that, but we want to *very* much.

Walking downstairs to the baggage carousel, we stand there hand-in-hand waiting. My one bag comes out quickly - for the first time ever!

When we reach the moving walkway that goes to the parking garage, I let you go first. As you step on, I take a good look at you. You're wearing a long skirt that comes down past your knees, leather boots, and a very nice jacket with a beautiful embroidered pattern all over it. Underneath that, you have on a knit blouse that buttons up the front. I imagine myself undoing those buttons and wonder if you eventually might let me?

We take the elevator to the 5th floor of the parking garage. I'm curious about what kind of car you drive and also notice there are hardly any other vehicles parked on this level. Your stylish boots click,

click, click as we walk all the way across the parking area towards the farthest corner. As we come to a brand-new white luxury SUV, I think to myself. "Wow!"

You push a button on your key ring and the rear hatch opens. I put my bag inside. You push another button and the rear hatch closes again. I turn around to find your arms wrapping around me. We hug tightly. Looking up at my face, you say "Kiss me!"

As our lips meet for the very first time, you take the lead and slip your tongue into my mouth - just a little bit. I respond and, as I do, feel your hands slide up underneath the back of my leather jacket.

Our eyes meet again after our first steamy kiss. I put my hands on your bottom and give it a playful squeeze. Your eyes twinkle while you push another button on your key remote and I hear a different door pop open. It's one on the passenger side, so we slowly walk that way.

I try to open the front passenger's door, but it's still locked. You silently point to the rear door on that side. I open it and you get into the back seat first. Following you in, I notice that it's all beige leather and carpet inside, with blackout windows all around - nice!

I'm still a bit puzzled, but things become instantly clear as you lean back on the huge leather seat, spread your legs, and motion to me to move in between them. Your long skirt still covers your legs down to your knees. Placing one palm on each of my cheeks, you pull my lips towards yours.

This time, I'm the aggressive one. I kiss you firmly, then lightly lick your lips in a teasing kind of way. As we kiss again, you slowly move your knees apart. Our chests press closer and closer together. Your hands return to my leather jacket and help me to take it off.

Playfully tossing it into the front seat, you remove your jacket and toss that into the front seat too. It lands on top of mine.

I kiss you again and whisper. "You beautiful, sexy woman - how I've waited for this moment!"

"Yes, me too!" you agree.

Now is the moment that we've both been anticipating. My fingers unbutton the top button of your knit blouse, then the second, then the third.

Slipping one hand inside your blouse, I'm delighted to discover that you aren't wearing a bra. My fingers lightly brush across your left nipple while you unbutton the last two buttons of your blouse yourself. You push your chest out to proudly display your lovely bare breasts. Smiling, anticipating, you run your fingers through my hair as my head moves down.

I take your right nipple into my mouth. It hardens instantly. Then I kiss your left nipple - it's already excited.

You begin pulling at your skirt. As you pull it up a bit more, I can feel how smooth your legs are. Each inch that you hike up your long skirt allows me to move an inch closer to you. My dress pants are getting way too tight in the front.

Slowly, slowly, you keep pulling up your skirt. Then you stop. Sliding your hands under the front of my cashmere sweater, you quickly take it off over my head. I lean forward and your bare breasts brush against my bare chest. Your warm, hard nipples feel wonderful! My pants are about to burst at the seams.

You whisper into my ear. "Could you please straighten up a bit?"

As I do, your fingers unbutton the front of my pants and unzip my zipper. You're surprised to see that I have no underwear on. It seems that we've both gone "commando" in anticipation of this moment!

My cock is almost fully erect for you now. Encircling it with your fingers, you pull it towards your hungry mouth. As your moist lips wrap around the head, I moan softly. You swirl your tongue around and around the tip of it, then suck as much as you can into your mouth -

wetting and warming it. Mmmmmm!!!

Without warning, you push my cock down towards your raised-up skirt. As I look down, your free hand hikes your skirt up the rest of the way and I see that you have no panties on. Not only that, but I can see that you're already dripping wet!

Your soft, warm fingers lead my cock right to the opening of your lovely pussy. Then you slide your whole body forward on the seat and instantly take part of it inside. Your eyes are half-closed now and you look so damn sexy!

Spreading your legs even wider, you surrender yourself to me as much as you would for any man. I realize how lucky I am to have such a gorgeous woman want me!

You feel my cock start moving in and out - halfway in, all the way out, three-quarters in, all the way out, almost *all* the way in! You make a noise like a purring tiger.

Placing both of your hands firmly on my rear, you take a deep breath and pull my giant erection into your tingling pussy as far as it will go. Now you can feel the tip of my cock pressing into your deepest places.

A single word escapes your lips. "Damn!!!"

Now I'm thrusting in hard and deep. With each stroke you're getting hotter and hotter - and wetter and wetter.

Each time I push, you push back. Our eyes meet again. As they do, you begin to cum - just a tiny little orgasm. You want more.

I'm still pumping, still thrusting - harder, deeper! My stiff cock is being washed with your cum and this drives me wild! I can't hold back any longer!

"May I cum inside of you, please?" I ask urgently.

"Oh, yes!" you say irresistibly. "That's *exactly* what I need to feel!"

I begin to slide *all* the way in, *all* the way out, all the way in - over and over again. Deeper, harder, faster, *faster!*

You give out a tiny scream as I push all the way in and just hold there - flexing my cock muscles. Your pussy muscles involuntarily flex back. Doesn't that feel wonderful?

All of a sudden, you're cumming again! Your hips move excitedly from side-to-side as I push in and pull out. The look on your face say it all - we are definitely lovers now!

We kiss and hold each other for a long time there in the back seat, just enjoying being in each other's arms.

After several delicious minutes of this, we realize that we're very hungry and help each other to get dressed. As we step out to move to the front seats, you toss me the keys.

"Why don't you drive, please?" you ask. "I might need you to finger my pussy while we're on the parkway."

We both laugh - and just think - all the rest of our romantic weekend is still ahead of us!

Licking You

Because you're such a beautiful and sexy woman, you deserve to have special attention given to all of your needs. Stretching out on the sofa, you feel my lips on yours as my long fingers gently touch your nipples through your blouse. As they become more and more aroused, my fingers slip inside of your bra to feel how hard they are with desire.

Quickly unbuttoning your blouse, I unhook your bra and tease you by kissing all around the edges of your breasts until you just can't take it any longer and ask. "Please kiss my nipples now?"

Moving your chest towards my face, you offer one nipple to my waiting mouth. I kiss it and suck it gently, then you place the other hard nipple against my lips. I kiss it also - taking it all the way into my mouth just the way you like it. Feeling my warm lips teasing your nipples increases both your passion and the wetness between your legs.

You unzip your jeans and hear me ask. "Are you ready for my tongue now?"

Silently, you help me take off my shirt, then motion to me to lie down on my back on the bed. Quickly removing your last articles of clothing, you position yourself so that one leg is on each side of my head.

Looking down, you see my smiling face between your legs and realize that this turns you on completely! My lips are only inches away from your lovely pussy. Your smooth inner thighs brush against my freshly-shaven cheeks. Moving both hands between your legs, you spread your pussy lips open and slowly sit down onto my waiting tongue. The first feeling of it touching your clit makes you gasp just a bit!

You begin to move your hips back and forth while pressing down farther and farther onto my tongue - back and forth, back and forth.

Now you close your eyes. Each time you slide forward, my tongue slips inside your opening. Each time you move back, it licks across your fully-aroused clit. You're making love to my tongue. Any shyness you might have felt disappears as you're on the verge of your first orgasm of the evening.

"Oh! I'm so damn close!!!" you blurt out without slowing down your frantic movements. "I'm going to fuck your tongue until... Oh! Oh!! Dammit, I'm cummmmming!!!"

I can feel your pussy muscles contracting around my tongue, then relaxing, then contracting again as your orgasm continues for what seems like forever. My face is soaked with your juices and your cum. I love it!

After a few moments, you regain control and kiss me in a way that lets me know how much you love to be licked.

"Now it's your turn!" you declare as your fingers unzip my zipper.

Night Nurse

I'm in bed in my private room at the hospital - not really sick, just having some routine tests. I do have to stay overnight for observation, though.

It's the beginning your night shift. You come in from the cold evening air, sit next to me on the bed, and give me an unusually friendly smile. I'm quite surprised by all of this because we've never met.

Next, you completely surprise me by throwing off the sheets and climbing up on top of me in the bed! Your uniform is chilled and temporarily gives me goosebumps as you mount my naked body.

As you line my nipples up exactly with yours, I can feel your full breasts straining against your tight uniform blouse.

"Who is this woman?" I wonder. "She certainly is aggressive!"

You kiss me deeply, sucking my tongue into your mouth as a sweet hello. I decide to just go for it and run my fingers through your hair as we share a long, passionate kiss. My hands move to the back of your smooth, cool uniform and firmly grip your ass. As you spread your legs and mount me with all of your clothes on, your white skirt rides up.

"I don't really want to stand up again to take off my nylons." you say urgently while raising yourself just enough to grab the front of them with both hands and rip them apart at the seam.

"Don't worry - I have another pair in my bag to finish my shift." you laugh.

After I help you to undo the bottom buttons of your uniform, you position yourself with the tip my cock touching the front of your panties. Smiling, you pull them aside and I feel a drop of moisture drip from your pussy onto my waiting cock.

"You're already wet?" I ask.

"Oh, yes! The nurse on the day shift texted me that it was all that she could do to keep her hands off you, and I'm not going to make the same mistake!"

After using your fingers to lubricate the tip of my cock with some of your juices, you start to take it inside. Mmmmmm - that feels great! I've never had sex with a nurse in a hospital before!

You begin rocking up and down on my cock while telling me how good it feels. Suddenly, without warning, you push down *hard*, and take in almost the whole thing! With a gasp of pleasure, you begin riding me like there's no tomorrow. I feel the need to get those panties off soon.

Not wanting to take my cock out of

your pussy, even for a moment, I tear off your panties and what's left of your nylons.

Squeezing your ass with both hands, I plunge my huge cock in as far as it will go. You feel an orgasm rapidly building. I help you by pushing down firmly over and over again.

One of your uniform buttons pops off as we move against each other like a couple of untamed animals. We don't really notice - all we're aware of is the rhythm of our lovemaking. Looking up, I see your breasts bouncing up and down with every movement we make.

"Please take off your blouse and bra?" you hear me ask.

You quickly do so and lean forward to press your bare breasts against my cheeks - feeling my hungry kisses between them as you ride me. I'm having trouble breathing, but I don't care.

Leaning back, you breathlessly whisper. "Slip your fingers in next to your cock and spread me wide open!"

I do what you ask and am surprised that it makes you cum almost immediately.

"Ohfuckyesssssssss!!!" you cry out while cumming wildly. "Fuck me *really* hard now!!!"

You feel me thrust as far in as possible. We're moving together as one and completely lost in pleasuring each other. Your bare breasts are bouncing against my chest, your tongue is in my mouth, and my cock is *way* deep inside of you. I feel like I'm going to explode, but try to hold off so you can cum again first.

You sit straight up so that no part of you is touching me except for your pussy lips. Your pussy kisses my throbbing cock and rides up and down my thick shaft. I love the look on your face as we keep moving together with nothing held back.

Leaning forward, you kiss me again. I pause on the very edge of orgasm - pulling you down onto me so I can feel flesh-to-flesh contact with every inch of your sexy body. Your excited movements tell me that you're also very close.

"Kiss me while we cum, lover." I say as my sperm rises for you.

Our lips meet, then our tongues. Your kisses are full of fire as if you are *trying* to make me cum - and you *do*!

We both explode with intense pleasure! You feel my hot sperm filling you as you squeeze my cock tightly with your pussy muscles.

******

"That was wonderful - my knees are weak!" you tell me as we hold each other. "I'm so glad that no one walked in on us!"

You snuggle up closer with your bare leg over mine, your arm across my chest, and your head on my shoulder.

"What's that I'm lying on? Oh - a uniform button!" you giggle. "It must have popped off at some point - I didn't even notice it before!"

I see a special sparkle in your eyes that can mean only one thing - total satisfaction.

"I'm getting discharged in the morning - will you come and visit me at home?" I ask hopefully.

"Oh yes, I'll take good care of you at home and will gladly lick your, er, wounds."

"I was only in for a checkup - and certainly got that!" I joke. "I wonder what you'll write on my chart about this? Maybe it will give the head nurse an eyeful!"

"I already know what I'll write." you tell me. "Patient is resting comfortably after full assessment of cardiovascular and respiratory functions. Will follow up after discharge with additional physical therapy for strengthening and endurance. Patient does not seem to be sleepy at all and has a quirky smile."

"You might have to give me an oral examination and of course, I'll reciprocate." I laugh. "You've made me very hungry! Shall I ring for the floor nurse?"

"I'd be so fired if she saw us like this!"

We both laugh.

"What's this?" you ask, reaching under your left shoulder. "Oh, another uniform button! It looks like I have some quick sewing to do!"

"I'm glad that you work the night shift."

"Me too!"

"And I'm afraid I've torn your white panties to shreds!"

"Oh, I didn't need them anyway," you giggle. "and no one but you will know that I'm not wearing any."

My Sexy Dream About You

I want to tell you about the sexy dream I had about you while it's still fresh in my mind.

You were wearing a see-thru white silk negligee and kind of floating above me as if you were on a cushion of air. I was lying on my back in the bed and we were face-to-face.

The white silk contrasted beautifully with your hair. I could clearly see your attractive nipples through the thin silk. Your hair touched my face as you kissed me - very gently at first, as though you were trying not to wake me.

As you kissed me more and more passionately, you lowered yourself very slowly onto my body. I felt your arms touch my shoulders, then your breasts touched my bare chest. Your firm nipples brushed against mine.

I felt your smooth legs straddle me - one on each side of my sleeping body. Your negligee was gone now and I could feel the warmth between your legs as your whole lower body made contact with mine.

Your sweet kisses had already begun to aroused me while I slept. I felt your warm fingers wrap around my shaft and move it up between your legs. Then you began to rub the tip of my cock ever-so-gently against your clit.

After a minute or so, you were completely wet. Your fingers gripped my shaft tighter as you spread your legs wider. Guiding the tip of my excited cock to your opening, you took just a couple of inches inside. Next, you rubbed the tip against your clit again, then back to your opening - taking 4 or 5 inches inside this time.

Whispering my name, you began rotating your hips in small circles as you took more and more of my big cock inside of your hungry pussy.

I could hear your breathing becoming heavier and feel your soft, warm skin against mine. Then you began to sway your hips from side to side. I could tell you were getting closer and closer to cumming because you began to moan - soft, sweet moans that really turned me on!

Each time you pushed down onto my throbbing cock, I pushed back. We were wildly making love! Before long, I felt your inner muscles tense and then a flood of your wet warmth surrounded my cock.

"I'm cumming!" you whispered.

******

It was a delicious dream! I only wish it

had lasted another few minutes because it was almost a wet one!

I woke up with a full-on erection and reached for my phone to call you. What a sexy way to begin the day!

You Take Charge

"I feel like taking charge of our lovemaking tonight," you tell me with a gleam in your eye. "so please sit in that chair over there."

I'm used to making the first move, but it excites me to know that you're feeling that way. I move to the big easy chair and sit down.

You walk over like a woman with a purpose, remove my belt, and put one hand on each side of my jeans.

"Lift up a bit." you say with a smile.

As I do, you pull my jeans and boxer-briefs down my muscular thighs, below my knees, and off. Folding them neatly, you place them on the arm of the chair, then take off my t-shirt. It also gets folded and joins my jeans and underwear. The red velvet of the chair feels good against my bare skin.

Taking a couple of steps back, you undo the buttons on the front of your jeans. Leaning down, you remove your socks and slide your jeans down - and off. They are also folded neatly and added to the expanding pile of clothes on the arm of the chair. Next, you grab the bottom edge of your t-shirt and pull it off over your head with the same vigor as you did mine. I notice right away that you don't have a bra on. You fold your t-shirt and add it to the growing pile.

Now you are standing before me naked, except for your robin's-egg-blue panties. Playfully slipping one hand inside of them, you dip one finger in between your pussy lips and place it into your mouth. You tease!

"Would you like to taste my pussy juice?" you ask with a devilish grin while putting your finger back inside of your panties.

Taking two steps closer to me, you rub your wet finger on my lips. I open my mouth and you push it in gently. It tastes great!

"Want more?" you ask while stepping out of your panties and putting one leg up onto the arm of the chair. This brings your lovely pussy only a few inches away from my face.

"Lick it!!!" you instruct me.

How can I refuse? You know how oral I am! In a hot minute, you feel my tongue doing exactly what you want.

As I lick, you reach down into my lap and begin to stroke my cock. It quickly responds and grows to fill your warm hand.

After a few minutes of eager licking, you ask "Let's move to the bed, OK?"

Taking me by the hand, you lead me to our big, comfortable bed. After easing me back onto my pillow, you lean down to kiss me.

You climb onto the bed and into my waiting arms. I can tell that you want me, and you know for certain that the feeling is mutual.

Since you want to be in charge tonight, you get on top of me. Sliding my hands up between your legs from behind, I touch your pussy. You feel my cock growing even bigger against your tummy as my fingers are exploring. We kiss. I put one of my legs between yours and rub it against your pussy. I can feel your wetness on my leg.

After a couple of minutes of this, you move to hover your ever-so-moist pussy right above the head of my cock, but not quite touching it. I love it when you take charge! You slowly lower yourself until we barely make contact.

I try to push inside of you, but you move up so I can't. My fingers move up to your breasts and gently pinch your taut nipples.

We both glance down and see ourselves poised for lovemaking. My huge cock is throbbing in your hand. Your pussy is already dripping with anticipation. Deciding that the time for teasing is over, you sit down forcefully! You can feel my hardness massaging your inner walls - it feels like heaven!

My hands are still on your hips. I give a mighty downward push. Your clit rubs along my shaft as you spiral down - squeezing, pulsing, enjoying every inch as it sinks deeper into your tight pussy.

Leaning over next to my ear, you make your needs known. "Make me cum."

Your pussy squeezes my cock, releases, and squeezes again - even tighter. I push harder and you push back.

"I need to feel your sperm explode into me!" you loudly declare as you sit all the way down and just hold there. Your pussy is calling my sperm. My cock is calling your cum.

You are panting now. That beautiful sound sends me right over the edge! My cock explodes for you in slow motion and fills your pussy with cum. More big gushes of sperm bring you closer and closer until you cum loudly!

"Damn! Damn!! Damn!!!" is all that you can say.

You want to kiss me, but are still out of breath. My hands brush from the back of your knees up to your shoulders and back again. This seems to calm you. Finally, you're able to regain your composure and we kiss.

"I'm going to sleep on top of you like this tonight," you say with authority "and in the morning you're going to make me buttermilk pancakes."

"You really *do* enjoy taking charge sometimes, don't you?" I reply with amusement.

Masturbating Together

After you replied to my ad on a well-known internet site, we decide to meet to try something that's a new experience for both of us - mutual masturbation.

You answer the door in your bathrobe. We hit it off right away.

After talking and laughing a bit, you suggest that we get more comfortable. Sitting at one end of the sofa, you touch your breasts through your thick robe while watching me take off all of my clothes except for my black boxer-briefs.

As you watch me undress, your smile gets bigger and your other hand begins to caress your bare legs. Almost naked, I sit at the other end of the long sofa facing you.

"We can masturbate together, but we can't have sex or even touch each other." you say coyly. "I have a boyfriend."

"I understand completely, but it won't be easy." I agree.

You smile and begin by putting one finger into your mouth and sucking on it suggestively. I smile back at you and rub my hands from the top of my chest down across my flat stomach to tease you.

Looking down towards where my hands are headed, you take a deep breath and squeeze your robe-covered breasts tightly with both hands..

The bulge in my underwear is definitely getting larger now. As my hands reach my groin, you slip one hand inside your robe to tease your left nipple. Your other hand moves from the outside of your smooth thigh to the inside. As you do this, your robe opens just a bit at the bottom. My gaze moves just for an instant from your eyes to that special place between your long, smooth legs.

Knowing that I'm looking, you slowly open the bottom of your robe farther and move your slender fingers up until they come to rest over your pussy - hiding yourself from my view. You are teasing me back and I love it! Now my cock is so big that it's poking out the top of my boxer-briefs.

Smiling, you let the top of your robe fall open to reveal your beautiful breasts. You're clearly proud of your body, and well you should be!

You unfasten the belt of your robe and let it fall from your shoulders. Now you're completely naked and very turned on.

Looking directly into your eyes, I pull my underwear down - and off. My right hand moves to stroke my hard cock as you put your right hand between your legs and begin massaging your pussy. In no time, you're wet enough to slip one finger inside.

Turning more towards me, you make yourself more comfortable. Putting one leg up onto the back of the sofa, you dip a second finger into your lovely pussy.

I turn to face you and wrap my fingers around my thick shaft. Each time you push your fingers inside your pussy, I stroke down to the base of my cock. Each time you pull your fingers out, I stroke up to the tip.

Now we're both getting very excited! You start moaning softly in the most beautiful, womanly way. Your eyes are half-closed, but are still looking into mine. From where you sit you can see the whole front of my naked body. You move your other leg to almost touch mine - but not quite.

In a few more minutes, we've both lost all of our inhibitions. My cock is throbbing. Your pussy is soaking wet. We both want more, *much* more.

Breaking your own rules, you move over next to me and run your fingers through my hair while looking into my eyes. Our lips meet - gently at first. Then you become very aggressive - like a woman who hasn't had sex in a long time. The next thing I know, your head is moving down and your full lips are wrapped around my cock.

"Mmmmmmmft!" you say with great

pleasure as you almost swallow it whole.

"Please turn turn around so I can lick you too?"

You give my cock one more big slurp before turning around to offer your pussy to my tongue. We move into "69" position.

Putting my face between your thighs, I take a good look at your beautiful pussy and dive right in. You feel me licking on either side of your clit as you lick up and down the full length of my cock..

My tongue touches your clit for the first time. You begin stroking my cock with your hand while sucking my balls into your mouth and gently caressing them with your tongue.

Spreading your pussy with my wet fingers, I place my lips firmly on your clit and start french-kissing it. Your hips begin to move involuntarily.

You're moaning with pleasure as you deep-throat as much of my cock as you can. I respond by driving my tongue as far into your insatiable pussy as it will go. Spreading your legs even farther apart, you squeeze my tongue rhythmically with your pussy muscles while suck-stroking my cock in an orgasmic frenzy.

My tongue has a mind of it's own - licking you wildly as you cum. I feel an unavoidable urge to cum in your mouth.

"Cum on my tongue while I cum in your mouth!" you hear me say forcefully.

"Fuck my tongue, you sexy woman!"

Still I'm licking, licking - massaging your clit with my tongue. We both hear the couch squeaking in time with our oral lovemaking. My cock about to explode.

You're still cumming wildly and grinding your pussy so hard against my face that I can't really breathe.

Sucking *all* of my big cock into your mouth, you deep-throat it again. Before you know it, you're swallowing hot gulps of my cream.

All of our senses are overwhelmed by our powerful orgasms. You cum again and again.

******

As we relax in each other's arms, you reach down to gather some of your pussy juice on your finger, wet my lips with it, and kiss me.

"I just couldn't keep myself from touching you," you confess. "and in a few minutes, I'm going to fuck you."

"Don't worry." I laugh. "Your boyfriend will never find out."

Two At Once

Coming home from work early, I unlocked the front door and entered the living room.

Our place was very quiet - almost *too* quiet!

Listening closely, I thought I could hear faint sounds coming from somewhere nearby. There seemed to be a soft thumping noise mixed with what sounded like a woman whispering.

"It must be the neighbors." was my first thought.

As I walked towards the kitchen to get some cold water, something red caught the corner of my eye. There, on the first step leading to the upstairs, was a red bra! I knew right away that it was too small to be yours. Two steps up from the mysterious bra was a small pair of red satin panties!

My curiosity was getting aroused. Standing at the bottom of the stairs, I looked up and saw a black lace bra on the fifth step! That one appeared to be just about your size.

The next few steps held two t-shirts (one small and one medium), two pairs of rumpled jeans, and a pair of black panties.

"I'll get water later." I thought to

myself. "What's going on here?"

Quietly climbing the stairs, I heard muffled sounds coming from our bedroom and tiptoed closer.

******

Reaching the partially open bedroom door, I can see that your former college roommate Sarah is lying naked on her back on the bed with her little legs hanging over the edge.

You are naked too. As you kiss up the insides of her thighs to her pussy lips, Sarah spreads her legs wider. While beginning to lick her clit, you slide your hands up to her small breasts and tease her perfectly-formed nipples until they are completely hard. Neither of you notice me entering the room.

I sit down in the big easy-chair to watch as you kiss up Sarah's flat tummy and take her nipples into your mouth - first one, then the other. She reaches down between her legs and slides one finger into her pussy. You slip your tongue in her mouth. She really seems to like that!

Sarah reaches down between your legs, starts rubbing your clit, and pushes one tiny finger just a little ways inside of your pussy. Then she pushes a second finger inside. You begin to slowly move your hips - fucking her fingers. All this time, you're kissing each other.

I'm sitting in the chair watching and getting more and more aroused. Soon, my cock is fully-erect for both of you.

Rolling over onto your back, you flip Sarah over on top of you. She moves her head down between your legs and begins to lick your pussy while sliding her fingers in and out. The two of you are really going at it!

Unable to wait any longer, I silently take off all of my clothes and stand at the edge of the bed behind both of you. Sarah is lying on top of you now face-to-face and kissing you. Her fingers have returned to your pussy and you are grinding against them frantically.

Moving up behind you both, I touch my cock to Sarah's wet fingers as they fuck you. She jumps just a bit with surprise, wraps her tiny hand around my huge cock, and guides it to the opening of your ready pussy. After helping me push it an inch inside of you, her fingers return to rubbing her own hard clit.

You don't quite know what's happening at first, but soon you recognize the feeling of that cock you know so well and relax to allow more penetration.

Sarah keeps finger-fucking herself as I slowly push my huge cock deeper and deeper inside your pussy. Still the two of you are kissing.

Now I'm fucking you while Sarah is on top of you. I have a wonderful view of both of your sexy bodies intertwined and your soaking wet pussies just inches apart from each other and craving action.

I hear Sarah mumble between kisses. "Please fuck me some, too!"

Her wet fingers take hold of my cock again and move it from your pussy to hers. Her tiny pussy is so tight! It isn't easy for her to take very much cock just yet, so I gently move just the tip in and out so as not to hurt her.

Sarah is lying on top of you with her chest pressed against yours and her tongue still in your mouth. My huge cock is still between both of your legs as I continue to fuck Sarah. She's starting to moan loudly.

I can tell that you want me to fuck you more, too. Since you're both right there in front of me with your pussies fully accessible, I begin to go from Sarah's pussy to yours and back again.

First I push in and out of your dripping pussy ten times, then in and out of Sarah's tight little pussy ten times. Going back to yours, you feel me push in hard eight times. The last time I thrust *all* the way in as far as it will go. Moving back to Sarah's pussy, she feels my big cock pushing half-way in eight times.

Now you're both overcome with pure pleasure and still enjoying each other's kisses.

I continue to fuck you both - five times all the way inside of you, five times deeper inside of Sarah. She can take just a bit more cock with each long, smooth stroke.

Three times for you, three times for Sarah. You're both almost ready to cum. I'm getting close to cumming too, but not until you both of you do first!

I start rubbing the tip of my cock first against your clit, then Sarah's - going back and forth from one hot pussy to the other. Quickly now - faster, faster!

Suddenly, Sarah is cumming! I thrust my cock into her quivering pussy as far as it will go and hold it there - flexing my cock muscles to help intensify her orgasm. I can feel her hot cum oozing all around my shaft as she excitedly fucks me back. The noises that she's making turns all three of us on even more!

You've been fingering your clit while I fuck Sarah. You can feel her whole body moving against yours each time I stroke into her pussy. These motions and the sweet sounds of Sarah cumming bring you right to the very edge of your own orgasm. A moment later - you are cumming, too!

I drive my whole cock deep into your pussy and flex it while your hot cum flows as well. You're both making such lovely, sexy sounds!

Now I'm getting close to orgasm and begin to fuck you both again - first one long stroke deep inside of Sarah's pussy, then one deep inside of yours.

Sarah's, yours, Sarah's, yours, Sarah's. All of a sudden, you both hear:

"Unh! Unh!! Unhhhhhhh!!!"

My orgasm is a strong one. You feel my hot cum spraying all over both of your still-trembling pussies. Neither of you had the slightest idea that your lesbian love-making session might turn into this!

Sarah moves her hand down between your legs and rubs my fresh cum all over your pussy, then all over hers. Clearly, you both love to be soaked with cum.

After a minute, you move apart to let me lay down on my back between the two of you. First I kiss you long and hard, then I kiss Sarah.

Reaching down, I put one of my hands between your legs and one between Sarah's. You're both completely drenched with cum!

Sliding a finger into each of your pussies, I begin to rub both of your clits at the same time. Both of you are kissing my neck and feeling my still-hard cock. Soon, the motions of my fingers make you both cum again at exactly the same time.

"Oh!!!" you gasp as your cum squirts all over my hand.

"You sure make love to us like a man!" moans Sarah as her pussy muscles contract tightly around my finger.

Before I know it, you've both moved down and are kissing and sucking my cock at the same time. The feeling of two sets of wet, warm lips moving all around my shaft is more than I can take! In a couple of minutes you both watch as my cum shoots straight up in the air! It's the best orgasm that I've ever had!!!

"Thank you ladies for the wonderful surprise!" I say with appreciation.

"The surprise was ours!" you both answer at the same time.

******

Afterwards, we all lay naked together on the bed hugging, talking, and laughing until we realize that our lovemaking session has made us all hungry.

We all get into the shower together. Then I take both of you to a nice restaurant, where we all feel each other up under the table while talking about how and where we'll have our next threesome.

Seduction Massage

I'm not going to lie to you - I want to give you a sensual massage with every intention of turning you on so much that we just *have to* make love.

I'll begin by massaging your neck, shoulders, and lower back while you're lying on your stomach. This will get you used to my touch and let you know that I'm both gentle when you want me to be, and strong when you become filled with desire.

Doesn't the warm massage oil feel great as my hands effortlessly glide over your smooth skin? Do you like the soothing sound of my voice as I help you to become relaxed?

After a few minutes of this, I'll ask you to turn over onto your back so I can massage your arms. I'll cover your breasts and lower half with soft towels so you'll feel comfortable.

While you relax more and more, you'll feel my strong hands working on your hands, arms, and shoulders. When those areas are loosened up, I'll start massaging your upper chest and sides - all the while working ever-closer to your towel-covered breasts.

As your thoughts turn to pleasure, my

fingers will slip just barely under the edges of the towel - just a bit more with each pass. When your nipples are erect and longing for my touch, you'll feel my warm fingers lightly brush against them beneath the towel.

Then you'll hear me ask. "Would you like to leave the towel in place, or take it away?"

It's your choice - whichever you prefer. Either way, you'll feel my fingers keep brushing across your aroused nipples again and again until you're ready for the next step.

Taking both of your nipples between my thumbs and forefingers, I'll massage them lightly until your face tells me that you're enjoying my touch. Then you'll feel my strong hands glide down your tummy and back up your sides - over and over again. Each time they pass your erect nipples, my fingers will rub them with a little firmer pressure each time.

As you give clear signs of your increasing desire, I'll begin to massage your legs. You'll feel my fingers working on each toe, then your ankles, then slowly moving up to your knees. I'll massage down your outer legs, then up the insides of your thighs until you begin to spread your legs a bit more with each pass. This will be the signal that I'm looking for.

As your sexual tension builds, my

fingers will travel farther and farther up your inner thighs until you can feel them just barely brushing against the edges of your pussy under the towel. When your desire becomes too intense, you'll lose all inhibitions and spread your legs to give my fingers access to your whole pussy.

After a few more minutes of gentle rubbing, you'll hear me whisper again "Do you want to leave the towel on, or shall I remove it?"

Again, the choice is yours. You'll feel my fingers gently brush against your clit and move back down the insides of your thighs. Up to your clit, and back down - over and over again.

You're getting very aroused now. I can feel how warm and wet you are. A strong wave of horniness comes over you.

This will be a sign to me that you're ready for the next step of our erotic encounter. As my finger begins to rub all around the opening of your pussy, you'll feel my tongue lick up the insides of your thighs. When it finally reaches your pussy, you'll feel it wetting your clit.

Now you're completely aroused and your thoughts are turning to sex. By this time, you'll know that I'm an excellent lover who considers your pleasure to be *very* important. You look down to see that my cock is hard and thick and realize that I'm only waiting for your permission to move to the next level.

My tireless tongue has brought you to the edge of your first orgasm. Wrapping your fingers up in my hair, you hold my face firmly between your legs as you start to cum. Your hips begin to rotate excitedly as you press your soaking wet pussy *hard* against my face and tongue.

Suddenly, I can taste your cum! It tastes incredible!

You feel my muscular body moving up between your legs. Feeling my cock enter you at last drives you wild! You begin to rotate your hips in steady circles around my thick cock.

"Yes, you beautiful woman," you hear me whisper. "it's time to make love! Do you like being filled up completely by my big cock? Does it make you hot to think about it? Are you going to cum for me again?"

"Uh huh!!!" you exclaim. Your second orgasm is even stronger.

We kiss as you cum. Your hot kisses turn me on even more and you soon feel a spurt of my thick cum warming you to the very core.

We're lost in our lovemaking - kissing, caressing, thrusting - more slowly now as we enjoy the touch of each other's flesh.

******

Relaxing together on the massage table, our hands caress each other's bodies while we savor this special moment.

"You certainly have magic hands!" you tell me with a huge grin. "Thank you - I needed this so much!!!"

3 AM

It's 3 am. A cool breeze blows in the window and across my naked body as I awaken from a peaceful sleep. I move over to snuggle into your warm arms, but you're not there.

Rolling out of bed, I slip on my night shirt and walk towards the living room. Nearing the open door, I can see that the TV is on with the volume turned way down low.

I peek in. It appears that the cable movie that you're watching has only just started, although the policeman already has the hot blonde "spread eagled" on the hood of his cruiser. He's unbuckling his belt as she tells him that she'll do *anything* if he'll just let her off with a warning. I watch from the doorway as you untie your robe belt and settle back onto the couch.

Tiptoeing towards the back of the couch, I see that you have your favorite vibrator in your hand and are touching it between your legs while watching the screen intently.

Leaning in to kiss your neck, I whisper. "A little late-night action, eh?"

You turn and smile shyly - like a little girl caught with her hand in the cookie jar.

"I couldn't sleep." you explain. "The moonlight was shining on your sleeping body and I got horny. I wanted to jump on top of you, but didn't want to wake you."

You don't seem to realize that you're rubbing your vibrator against your clit while explaining. I find myself getting turned on by your actions.

Still standing behind you, I begin to massage your shoulders as we watch the blonde drop to her knees and take the policeman's little cock into her mouth.

"She's pretty hot," I comment. "and I'm imagining *you* in that position right now."

You give me your most inviting smile. I walk around the couch and unbutton my night shirt as you watch. I stand slightly off to one side so you can still see the action on the TV screen.

Leaning in, I take your head in my hands and kiss you - slowly sucking on your bottom lip as you sit there with your vibrator still in your hand. You reach up to pull me closer, but I resist and give you a sexy little smile.

Deciding to play along with the movie, I say. "Not yet, you lawbreaker! You need to give me a reason to let you off with just a warning."

I open my night shirt to reveal that my cock is growing rapidly.

"Oh, officer!" you say while eyeing my manhood. "Your cock has grown quite a bit! Now it's time to let *me* take control."

Taking my cock in your hand, you pull it closer to your mouth. Your warm fingers stroke it while your tongue licks all around the tip. You pause for a moment and seem to be thinking.

The next thing I know, you hungrily gobble up almost the whole thing!

"Where did you learn to suck cock like *that*?" I ask between quick, short breaths. "If you keep that up, you're going to make me cum in only three minutes!"

You're still watching the TV out of the corner of your eye. The blond has both hands on top of the police cruiser and her legs spread wide. The cop has moved in behind her.

While continuing to suck my cock, your fingers move down between your legs and touch your clit. Spreading your knees apart, you slip one finger inside of your pussy. Still you are sucking. As the policeman abruptly shoves his tiny cock into the blond woman's pussy, you reach for your vibrator.

"You won't be needing that tonight." you hear me say.

"Oh, no?" you ask coyly. "Why not?"

"Because we're going to make love now," I reply. "not just fuck like those people on the TV."

Your eyes light up. "Can we do it from behind? You know how much I enjoy being on all fours! I love that position because your huge cock gets in good and deep!"

Reaching for the remote, you turn off the TV. This tells me how much you want it!

Taking off your robe, you get down on all fours, look around, and give me that special smile that only you can give.

I kneel behind you, place the tip of my cock between your legs, slip the first inch into your pussy and just hold it there. I'm wondering - if I remain motionless, will you back up onto it or wait for me to push in farther?

It doesn't take long to find out the answer! I watch half of my cock disappear into your pussy as you back up onto it. Then you pause as if you aren't quite ready to take any more.

Sensing that you need to be wetter, I lick two of my fingers, reach between your legs, and moisten your clit. Almost immediately, I can feel your pussy getting wetter and am able to push another couple of inches inside. A bit more clit rubbing allows you to take almost all of it.

You begin to move against me - forward until just the tip is inside, then back until you've taken in more than half. Forward until just the tip is inside, back until three-quarters of my big cock is inside. Still my wet fingers massage your clit.

Rocking steadily back and forth, you're making love to yourself with my thick cock and thinking how much better it feels than your vibrator. Youre now able to take in my whole cock with each stroke - all 9 inches of it. We move against each other - pushing, pulling, making sweet love.

All of this stimulation brings you to that special place you can never quite remember until you're there - those unique feelings that overtake your senses just before you cum.

I pull out all of my stiff cock except for the very tip and slowly, slowly push it back in. You want to thrust back against it hard, but you're so close to cumming that you're unable to move.

Slowly, slowly, you feel it push inside - one inch, two, four, six, eight. Rocking your whole body back, you take in the last inch - and just in time, too!

"Oh my god, yessssss!!!" you blurt out while feeling the first thick spurt of my cum shoot forcefully into your pussy.

My slippery fingers move back to your clit and massage it more aggressively. I'm still pumping you from behind.

Your eyes are closed and your head is thrown back with pleasure. We have the perfect rhythm going. You wiggle your hips in a frenzy - and gush! I sink my cock in as far as possible and hold completely still as you keep cumming.

******

Our knees are weak.

"Please lie on your back?" you hear me ask - and you do.

I lay down beside you. Lifting up one leg, you take my cum-washed cock in your hand and help it back inside of you. We kiss.

Your fingers move to where we're joined together - feeling my cock surrounded by your still-trembling pussy.

"Lover?" I whisper.

"Yes?"

"The next time you wake up horny in the night, please wake me up instead of watching some tacky TV sex movie, OK?"

"Yes, you *know* I will!"

In the Backyard Hammock

It's the hottest day so far this Summer and we're lounging together in your backyard hammock.

Up until this point our relationship has been friendly, but not very physical except for hugs, casual kisses, and occasional snuggling. Lately though, you seem to be becoming more and more attracted to me, and I definitely feel the same way.

We're laughing and sharing a tall glass of a refreshing fruit drink - one glass, two straws. You have your arms wrapped around me and I'm putting your straw to your lips. The red fruit punch makes your lips look even rosier than usual. You smile and playfully touch them to my neck.

I shiver and say. "Wow! That's cold, but I like it!"

Taking a sip of the cold drink, I teasingly press *my* lips against *your* neck. You jump, then hold your neck against my lips - enjoying how the coolness takes your mind off the heat of the day.

We both sip. Now both of us have cold lips. Isn't that a great feeling? Especially on such a hot day!

I playfully kiss your forehead, the tip

of your nose, and down to your mouth. It's definitely starting to get hotter in the hammock. You look into my eyes as I hold the glass up for you to drink again.

This time you take the straw between your lips, but you don't drink. Instead, you move your tongue in tiny circles around the end of the straw. Then you take a small sip, making a loud slurping noise as you do. You're teasing me and I love it!

You swallow and press your cool lips against mine. While we're kissing, I don't notice your fingers reaching into the glass and taking out an ice cube. As your kisses distract me, you let the ice melt between your fingertips.

You nibble on my lower lip and then whisper. "Kiss me harder, please?"

I do what you ask.

As I do, you slide your cold fingertips up under my shirt and touch them to my right nipple.

I jump! You really surprised me! (But I kind of liked it!) Moving your fingers around on my chest, they slowly warm up.

We kiss again, but this time you are more aggressive. I love your kisses and have always wanted more!

You seem to read my mind. Taking your hand out from under my shirt, you rest your head on my shoulder as we lie together in the hammock. Placing one arm across my chest, you cuddle up even closer. I can feel your breath on my neck.

I whisper. "You know what? I like this a *lot!*"

You say nothing, but move one of your legs up across both of mine, giving me a clear signal that you like it too. It feels great to hold each other, doesn't it? We aren't in any hurry and are just enjoying each other's company.

Squeezing me tight, you kiss my neck again. The hammock sways in the gentle breeze as you move your leg farther across mine. I can feel the warmth of your body along my whole side.

"Let's drink together again." you suggest.

Your lips wrap around one straw and mine around the other. We look into each other's eyes - both smiling as we drink. Then you take the glass from my hand and set it on the table next to the hammock.

Without saying a word, you move your whole body up on top of mine. Your eyes are sparkling with mischief. I've often dreamed that something like this might happen for us, but never thought that it actually could!

You kiss my forehead, my eyes, my cheeks - and as your tongue slips between my lips, you begin to unbutton my shirt. First the bottom button, then another -

and another. Your red lips still press against mine as you unbutton the last button.

Sitting up on top of me, you look down to where both of your hands are now caressing my chest. Brushing your fingertips across my nipples, you feel them respond to your touch. We both are completely comfortable and in no hurry.

I run my hands up your spine on the outside of your blouse. You squeeze your legs together around my torso to let me know you like it.

"You're such a beautiful woman!" You hear me whisper.

While studying my face, you run your palms up and down my chest. You've always been amazed at how long my body is. Indeed, my arms are as long as your legs. Everything about me is long and slender.

A thought comes to you - a thought that you haven't allowed yourself to have for a long, long time. Usually, you're the kind of woman who can easily control her urges, but today something has come over you - a strong feeling that you're unable to resist. Your fingertips move to the lowest button of your blouse. You slowly undo it, then another button - and another.

One last button holds the front of your blouse closed. Your fingers move to it, then pause. You touch one hand to my lips. I kiss your fingertips. We smile at each other. Straightening yourself up, your fingers return to that last button and slowly unbutton it. Folding your arms across your chest, you smile sweetly like a little girl. You're teasing me again!

Moving both hands to the edges of your blouse, you slowly open it. I'm still looking into your eyes - not quite sure what to think.

"It's OK to look." you reassure me.

My eyes move down to look lovingly at your beautiful bare breasts. As I look, your hands reach for mine and press my warm palms against your chest. Your nipples fit between my fingers as if they were made just for that purpose.

You whisper again. "Can I tell you a secret?"

"Please do!"

"I'd love to suck your cock, make it all hard, then have you fuck me for hours. Please?"

Hearing this instantly makes me want you right *here*, right *now*! We're both thankful that the many trees and thick bushes keep the neighbors from seeing into your yard.

Moving back a bit to sit on my knees, you touch your hand to the front of my shorts and feel what your words have done to my cock. Sliding your whole body farther down my legs, you lean forward and kiss the rapidly-growing bulge in my shorts. Then you slide your hand up one of the leg openings, and wrap your fingers around my thick shaft.

"Hmmmmm." is all you say as the fingers of your other hand are busily unzipping my zipper. You're smiling with anticipation.

You don't even bother to take my shorts off - you just pull them down a few inches. Then you sit up straight - looking down at my sizable erection as if you're deciding exactly how to proceed.

The next thing I know, your lips are wrapping around my cock and you're making those loud slurping noises again! It's not a straw you're sucking on this time!

Between moans, you hear me say. "I want to lick your pussy while you suck my cock, please!"

You giggle with your mouth full. I take that as a "yes".

Standing up by the side of the hammock, you step out of your shorts, take your panties off, and playfully brush them across my face. I can smell your juices on them. What a tease you are!

"It's been a long time since I've had sex - please be gentle with me." you say while studying my enormous erection and thinking about how good it'll feel inside of you. But first, you want to suck it while I lick your pussy.

I help you climb back up into the hammock and soon you have one leg on each side of my head. You can feel my breath against the insides of your smooth thighs.

Wrapping both hands around the shaft of my cock, you hold it just an inch away from your eager lips while lowering your pussy closer to my waiting tongue. As as the tip of my tongue splits your pussy lips, you wrap your moist lips around the end of my cock. You shiver as my tongue touches your clit for the very first time.

You quickly suck more of my cock into your mouth. I return the favor by sucking your whole clit into my mouth. This surprises you! You tense up for a moment, then force your head as far down on my shaft as possible.

"Oh, damn!" you hear me exclaim. "Your mouth is so *hot*! Fuck my tongue please?"

Around and around your hips move - riding my tongue. Up and down your lips go on my cock. Can you taste it throbbing for you, lover? Let me lick you even deeper! Your hips rotate around and around as you fiercely fuck my tongue.

In and out goes my cock between your lips.

In and out goes my tongue while pleasuring your pussy.

I can feel your inner muscles begin to quiver. Each time I lick, they quiver a bit more. Yes, lover, I do want to taste your cum!

The warmth between your legs is building.

"Do you like having a big cock in your mouth while getting your pussy licked?" I mumble with my mouth full.

Around and around you gyrate your hips in reply. Your pussy juices are running down the sides of my neck as you get closer and closer. Cum to me, lover! Cum on my tongue!

Abruptly, you stop moving your hips and take as much of my big cock into your mouth as you can. This tells me that you're close - *very* close!

"Cum in my mouth!!! Cum with me now!!!" I hear you say urgently.

As your pussy muscles contract around my rigid tongue, you suck hard and make even louder slurping noises than before. Your cum begins to flow at last!

A thick rope of my cum shoots into your mouth with such force that you swallow some in surprise! This makes your orgasm even stronger. Your cum runs down my cheeks and neck and onto the hammock beneath us.

"Fuck me now!" you demand loudly. "I've waited a *long* time for this!"

This is all the encouragement I need! Rolling you over onto your back, I turn your whole body around so your legs are hanging off the side of the hammock. In an instant you feel my cock pushing into your horny pussy.

Each time I thrust, the hammock moves a few inches away from my body - taking you with it. The momentum then swings you back against my stiff cock.

Looking down between your legs, you can see an inch or two more of my cock penetrating your pussy with each sway of the hammock. As you watch, you wonder if you could *ever* take *all* of it.

Your question is quickly answered as you watch me push, then take two small steps forward. The very next swing of the hammock drives my cock into your soaking wet pussy right up to the hilt!

"Ooooooooooohhhhh!!! Fuck me!!! Fuck me *good*!!!" you cry out.

I take another step forward and the hammock stops moving. You look down again to see that your pussy has completely swallowed up my massive erection! Bending towards you, I pick you up and start bouncing you up and down on my stiff cock while standing next to the hammock.

You can't really believe what's happening! Your legs are wrapped tightly around my waist. Your pussy is so full of cock that it couldn't fit even another half-inch. Your whole body is being moved up and down as if you weigh nothing.

All of these sensations come to a climax. Your toes curl, your pussy clenches involuntarily around my cock, and you hear yourself sing out with pure pleasure.

******

As we relax in the hammock, you reach for the cool glass of fruit punch, hold it between us, and offer me a straw. We drink to quench our thirst, then cuddle up into each other's arms.

You playfully stick your tongue out at me to show me how red it is from the punch. I do the same. Then we kiss in a loving, yet erotic way.

As you close your eyes and reflect on what's just happened, another thought comes to you - the thought that somehow you've grown through this experience. Your inability to resist your sexual urges has helped you to become a more sensual woman. No longer will you try to restrain those feelings when they arise. You've come to realize that you thoroughly enjoy sex!

About the Author

Rory Richards has been told that he's a cunning linguist. His hobbies include eating out, pearl diving, and doing the horizontal Mambo.

Rory has always shared a special bond with women and enjoys writing for them in a way that is both respectful and stimulating.

Many of Rory's stories arise from his vivid imagination. Some have been inspired by dreams and by suggestions of sexy situations from his readers. Others describe actual encounters.

20 Sexy Stories: Romantic, Erotic Stories For Women To Enjoy is a 3-book series of romantica. Written over a period of several years, these sizzling stories have been enjoyed by thousands of women around the world.

This collection of Rory's writing has finally been released as 3 separate books, each of which offers 20 different stories for your reading pleasure.

Currently single and living in Portland, Oregon, Rory enjoys dating, traveling, reading, hiking, canoeing, and experiencing all of the natural beauty that the Pacific Northwest has to offer.

Rory would like to thank his readers

for their many wonderful letters and emails. You can reach him at roryrichards10@yahoo.com

If you enjoyed reading this book, please consider writing a review.

Also By Rory Richards

Books

20 Sexy Stories: Book One

brings you 20 romantic, erotic stories that promise to arouse your passion including: A Knock at My Door, A Thousand Kisses, At the Movies, Dream Lovers, In Your Hotel Room, Out For a Drive, The Beach House, Under Your Desk, The Old Brass Bed, Your Birthday Surprise, and ten more !

20 Sexy Stories: Book Two

includes another 20 romantic, erotic stories that will stimulate your imagination including: Adventure in the Woods, At the Library, Early Morning, The Horsewoman, In the Guest Room, Lucky Accident, Lunch Hour, Quickie, In Your Sleep, You Like To Be On Top, and ten more!

Published in the United States of America

Printed in Great Britain
by Amazon